THE WOE OF

SHADOWS

HEAVY LIES THE CROWN PREQUEL

BY D. FISCHER

The Woe of Shadows (Heavy Lies the Crown: Prequel)

ISBN: 978-1-952112-44-7

I dedicate this book to my sister, Rachel.
You are a bright light to guide the way through the dark.

Everything in this book is fictional. It is not based on true events, persons, or creatures that go bump in the night, no matter how much we wish it were...

Contents

Chapter One

The Past

Amala can see Fate's form zip through the cobbled, multi-colored streets which wind, weave, and slope to homes, shops, and then finally the Shadow Kingdom castle. The street stones are an array of deep purple, dark blue, and shimmering sea green, uneven and warped by time.

In the Shadow Kingdom, these shades add the much-needed array of colors to brighten the kingdom that's stuck in an unending twilight. Amala had been observing the shine of her clean streets from her bedroom window within the castle when Fate's black and gold dots had caught her attention.

Though it's difficult to distinguish between night and day here, it is currently night. Most shadow people are shut in their homes and tucked in their beds, fast asleep. The morning will come soon enough, and everyone has their duties to attend to, shops to open, and many men plan to hunt the night creatures of the Shadled Forest before the sun rises in the Divine Realm.

These are only a small sum of the obligations that make the kingdom spin round. Most duties are exhausting, and the people under Amala's rule barely make it to their beds before they're fast asleep. Amala's duties are no exception. Exhaustion weighs on her heavily, but most of that could be due to her spike in hormones.

Although the people are hard-worked, it is a happy kingdom, and Amala loves her people. It's a home. It's a place of safety provided by their creator, Fate. But today. . .

Today, something feels different. This off feeling had brought her to the window in the first place. She's been standing here for several minutes, alternating between the view and pacing her room while she tries to work out this smothering atmosphere even her kingdom, sandwiched between the shadows that it is, can feel.

Amala's father, the former King of the Shadow people, Iseal, had passed away just days before from the natural cycle all life endures. Grief still presses on her chest, but she had promised him she would celebrate his passing, and not mourn for too long. After all, he was happy to go to the afterlife and be with his wife who had died when Amala was a child.

As next in line for the throne, Amala and her husband Davan Ashcroft took the oaths while the memory of her father's burning body still resonated in her mind. Once their oaths were voiced before the people, Amala became queen, and Davan became king, and their daughter, still growing in Amala's womb, had become Princess of the Shadow People.

Amala paces once more, waiting for Fate to come to her window like he always does when he has news to share. Her fingers trail circles around her swelling abdomen, and a nerve in her eyelid twitches to the stress of the day – to this wrong feeling blanketing the realm.

Shadow people have two forms: Their black skin that shines with the thousands of speckled little stars – a galaxy stretching across bones, muscle, and black skin – and their human form with pale white skin. The only feature remaining the same in either form is their bright white hair. Now, feet silently treading the royal master bedroom's floor, Amala wears her human form. Mostly, Shadow People don't wear their shadow form unless there is danger or they leave the safety of their kingdom.

Fate's lemon scent washes inside the room, and the lit torches burning along the walls sputter before they blaze to life once more. Amala turns to Fate and his hovering form of swirling black and gold dots. Her feet feel like lead as his emotions roll off him in waves and slam into her ever-present unease.

"Is it done?" Amala asks. She's almost afraid for the answer, for what he'll say next determines their future. Amala knew about the Realm's War, and she was thankful it did not reach the Divine Realm. At least, not yet.

"It is," Fate murmurs. His voice comes from seemingly everywhere, and yet nowhere, as if it's whispered in the wind and Amala's mind at the same time.

The queen breathes a sigh of relief, grateful she won't have to ask her people to join the Realm's War. It's selfish of her, she knows, but it's a war she had no interest in

9

aiding. She'll do anything to maintain the serenity of her kingdom and the joyful lives who live within it.

"Is it who we feared?" Amala asks. Her tone is tentative yet pressing. She glides closer to Fate, gathering her white hair and pulling it over one shoulder. The ends nearly touch her hipbone. "Was it Despair? Has he grown stronger?" Amala isn't sure she wants the answer.

There are four Divine gods who created all: Fate, Hope, Choice, and Despair. While none started out as good or bad but rather neutral, time has shaped them to be different from one another, rebellious and jealous. Hope and Choice remain largely unbiased and uninvolved, but Despair has grown thirsty to rule all. Once Fate had learned of Despair's goals, he had intervened, creating five chosen warriors to replace corrupt fee rulers of the other realms, effectively sparking the Realm's War.

In intervening the way he did, Fate knows Despair will destroy him. Despair had been close, so close to gaining control of the other realms. Despair had gone as far as possessing the Demon Realm's ruler, an unforgivable act, and in the end, it had nearly cost Fate everything.

"Yes," Fate answers with graveness that would make the stars tremble. He's exhausted, so exhausted, and it seeps through his voice. "And I fear the other realms were only a short-term goal in the schemes he's concocted. His end goal wasn't just to rule his children's realms but to rule them all." *Including this one*, Fate doesn't say, but the implications are there anyway.

"But he didn't this time," Amala says hopefully. She allows a breath of relief. "He didn't win."

"He was pushed back to this realm," Fate reveals.

Amala's shoulders sag. That's the off feeling Amala has felt all day. Despair is back on the Divine Realm. The other realms may be safe at this moment, but now the fight may become her responsibility anyway. Despair will need to be dealt with. Possibly ended. This isn't over, and Amala knows it. As Fate's prized creations, besides their Fee children who had once ruled the other realms, the Shadow People are where his heart truly lies. They are his blade, his just and merciful creations.

"Is the babe strong?" Fate asks. He knows the princess growing in her womb is healthy, but a change of subject is in order. He doesn't like seeing Amala in such a state.

There's a lump in the queen's throat, but she smiles past it and nods her head. The happiness is fleeting, however, and a solemn expression evaporates the grin. "What do we do? How do we stop him from taking over this realm? I can already feel him, Fate. I can feel his dark magic even in the shadows, such as we are. How do you know he won't come after you for meddling?"

"Oh, he will." Fate chuckles, but there's no real humor in it. "I do not know what the other Divine – Choice and Hope – have planned for their own survival, but I do have a plan of my own. In a way."

She cocks her head to the side, and her hair untwirls like a curtain from its twist. "How can I help?"

Fate is silent for a few moments, planning different scenarios. All lead back to one, however. One favorable outcome. One chance to save his realm.

Outside of the royal master bedroom, in the hall, chatter passes her doorway. Laughter, conversation, genuine ease in a kingdom where joy blossoms like a rose. They don't know. None of them do. They don't know what sort of future this kingdom will endure.

The burden Fate's about to dislodge from his shoulders and place on another's will be great, but for the survival of the Divine Realm and its people . . . well. Great sacrifices are the cost for such hope. Shadows can only be cast where there is light, and he's about to gift his light to another.

"Your baby."

Looking down, Amala scowls at her swelling stomach. Her nightdress is getting tight around her bellybutton, and soon she'll have to switch to a dress more appropriate for maternity.

"What of her?" Amala asks. Fate had told her once she conceived, Davan and Amala would be blessed with a girl. She'll have unimaginable strength, power, and responsibility. Amala had often wondered if Fate knew something of the future that Amala could never guess at. It would seem she was right.

Fate floats forward, hovering closer to the queen. Her nostrils flare at the lemon scent – a pure and clean aroma. "I will bless her with all that I am. I will give her myself."

"No!" Amala says. She shakes her head vigorously. "That will kill you." The Shadow People worship their creator. They love Fate more than they love their children, more

12

than they love themselves. What would the realms be without Fate?

"I will die anyway, but at least, fate can live on through her. The realms can live on through her. This realm – our realm – your people – will live because of her. Because of this one sacrifice."

Tears threaten to spring from the queen's eyes. She backs away, her hands protectively covering the baby in her womb. "I won't let you put that on a baby."

"Then your people will die."

She looks over at the bed large enough to sleep an entire growing family, then to the crown on the stand next to it. The crown is unique, made of crystals and twine and precious metals. Her late mother wore it when she was alive. The crown is only used when visiting other kingdoms, for the shadow crown, which can materialize on the royals' heads, is the one they normally adorn. Amala likes this crown, though she refuses to wear it. It stays on the nightstand like the relic it is. She feels like she has big shoes to fill, and by putting it on her head, it would somehow dishonor her mother's name and the good she had done for the kingdom. Only a few days into her reign, Amala knows she hasn't earned it. Not yet. Maybe she never will.

For a long while, she stares at it, watching the crystals wink and reflect the shimmering lights in the nearby hanging lantern. The lantern isn't full of fire, but of glowing Diabolus Beetles – large insects home to this land. Poisonous and deadly, just as many things of beauty are.

"We won't survive, will we?" she asks.

"I predict there will be many great losses in the coming years. Despair's wrath will not be pleasant."

"But my unborn – my daughter, Nefari – will? She will survive?"

"Yes. It shall be her fate." *Among other things,* Fate doesn't say.

Her hair sways as she nods slowly, sullenly. "Okay," she whispers. "Okay, do it."

"I am sorry, Amala. I am truly sorry. For all of it. But alas, this is not something I can manipulate and fix. I can fix much else, but not this. Giving Nefari myself is all I have left to give."

"I understand." Amala sniffles, and the knot in her throat forms once more. "Please," she beseeches. "Please, just get it over with."

Fate watches her for a moment longer, then presses his floating form closer to her abdomen. And then, Fate dives into the womb, merging. He can feel Amala's muscles tense with the intrusion, as she feels Fate circle the womb and press against the tiny soul within.

Fate feels relieved at what he finds: a powerful soul, one whose power is greater than her ancestors before her. It is the trait of the shadow royals to carry such power, to pass it down throughout generations, such as they do with the throne, but this level of magic Fate hasn't felt in a very long time. Possibly a twin to his own. This . . . This gives Fate hope for sacrifice. This gives him hope that he's not dooming a child to her own death. This gives him hope that all he has created on the Divine Realm will survive the days to come.

Chapter Two

Present Day

The bed sways a little when Amala Ashcroft sits upright from her dream. Automatically, she clutches the empty womb where her daughter, Nefari had once grown. She was safe, then. Secure. A tiny blip of flesh that would constantly nudge Amala's belly button.

The dream was a vivid memory of the last time she spoke with Fate before he gave his life for his people. Amala always has this dream when her daughter's birthday approaches. It's like clockwork, and it doesn't take a seer to understand why.

Sweat beads at her temple, and she swipes it away with the heel of her palm. The Queen of the Shadow Kingdom is worried for her daughter and for her people.

She looks to her hand, fingers clenching the thin silk nightgown while remembering the tightening feeling of Fate bestowing his power to her daughter. Seconds after the transference of power, she remembers the tremble of the Shadow Kingdom when Fate's volcano exploded, effectively announcing his demise. She remembers how it woke everyone, and the streets filled with weeping people when the suspicions of his death were confirmed.

She pushes her silky bright-white hair from her damp forehead, traces the hem of her silk sheets, and flexes her jaw. Irritation thunders through her, irritation at the dead god who created her people – the shadow people.

To put this responsibility on a child. A child! Her child! The grinding of her teeth is audible.

The scent of cinnamon and crisp winter air teases her senses as King Davan stirs next to her. She's always loved his unique aroma.

His white hair is slicked back, spiked at the back of the head, and shimmers gold under the smeared spotlight of the lone torch still lit in their chambers.

Swallowing thickly, she attempts to douse the rage building inside her echoed by the remnants of her dream's memory. She visually traces the stubble across his jaw, cheek, and chin. Davan's eyelashes are impossibly long, and she itches to kiss them. They always feel like feathers against her lips, a sensation worth repeating.

Davan rubs at his tipped ears and peeks vivid ice-blue eyes at her. "You're thinking about it again, aren't you?" he whispers, soft and loving.

Her husband had been part of the Onyx Guard when she had first stumbled across him. The Onyx Guard's chief job is to protect the shadow royals then protect their people. The Shadow People have an army – each shadow person is trained in the arts of all forms of combat – but the Onyx Guard goes through more extensive training.

She had been waiting at the entrance of the training room for Bastian, her centaur instructor, to arrive. Arriving early was unusual for her, so she had propped herself against the wall and observed the Onyx Guard's drill. She had watched Davan in a hand-to-hand training against three other men. None of the men had realized the princess was in attendance.

Amala had smirked when they had beaten him, of course, but Davan had put up an inspiring fight. Even more so, he took the criticism of his instructor well.

The princess was impressed and had asked to duel him the next day. Bastian had made sure she could protect herself if needed, and she was eager to put it to the test.

After a grueling match with wooden swords, she had bested Davan, and when his pride was not wounded, she had vowed to marry him someday. Bastian had not been happy about it. He felt she had dueled them to prove a point, but truly, she wanted to see what kind of man Davan was.

This sort of betrothal is unusual for shadow royals. Normally, their spouses are picked at a young age, and then the couple spends years courting one another, molding their personalities until they fit like a perfect, singular piece. Such a union symbolizes strength, which trickles down to the people.

Pulled from this memory by Davan rubbing warm fingers along her cooling back, she sighs. "How can I not think about it?" Amala whispers.

Instead of meeting her husband's gaze, she looks around at their possessions. Everything they own in their royal chambers was gifted to them by the villagers. Common drapes, two carved chairs built by a carpenter's apprentice, and a large fur rug made from many pelts. It was sewn together by a little girl whose dream is to someday design and sew a queen's gown.

Shadow People do not cherish wealth in currency but, instead, the wealth of their people. It is the Shadow Royals' duty to make sure their people have what they need.

"There's more to give than there is coin in this realm, Amala," her mother had once said. It had always stuck with her.

"Queen Sieba Arsonian –" Amala begins.

Davan pushes himself up into a seated position. The sheets fall from his bare chest, and his skin gleams in the dim light, just like his hair.

The king's knuckle brushes against her flushed cheekbone, and she peeks at him from under her lashes. "Queen Sieba cannot reach us, Amala. She cannot break through our shadows. The Shadled Forest has always protected us and will continue to do so long after you and I are gone from this realm."

He brushes his lips against Amala's. His lips are soft from sleep. "Not once in history has our enemy breached our shadow's protections. You needn't worry so much about it."

The Shadow Kingdom can only be entered by traveling through the Shadled Forest. The trees' shadows, to be exact. The entire village is surrounded by the creep, a foggy darkness which transports a living being from the kingdom to the Shadled Forest.

"You truly think our shadows will be enough?"

"It always has been."

Amala licks her lips. "That was before. That was when Fate was still alive. That was before the Realm's War when Fate had learned Despair possessed the Demon Realm's Fee and started a war across most of the realms, Davan." The young queen moves so she's face to face with her husband. "That was before when he was still alive. Before, Davan." *Before* is all she needs to utter. This conversation has been had time and time again in the last eight years.

"There are still two other divine gods that Despair will have to destroy before he can truly rule this realm, Amala." Davan's tone is impatient, and Amala bristles to it.

He had hoped with time, she would believe what he's telling her, but so far, the king has yet to get through to his queen. Davan stretches his neck, and the bones pop.

Amala grasps his hand gently. "No one has seen Hope and Choice for eight years, either. For all we know, they could have transferred their power to another as Fate had done to Nefari."

Davan barks a laugh and removes his hand from hers. "And who would they transfer their power to?" Davan didn't mean to raise his voice, nor does he like the hurt expression on Amala's face. He sighs, quiets his voice, and continues to push his point. "A pirate of Widow's Bay? A crone from The Frozen Fades? A slave from Urbana? Or perhaps a centaur of the Kadoka Mountains. Bastian, maybe? Choice loved his hooved creatures. Come now, Amala. You must see how ridiculous this sounds."

Amala's top lip curls, and she snarls at his belittling words. "Do not talk of the centaurs in such a way."

"Yes, yes, I know." He waves a hand in the air. "You're fond of them, too."

"They've agreed to help if Queen Sieba finds our kingdom. All I have to do is call upon them, Davan. That's more than I can say about you. At least they believe me."

Sliding from their bed, King Davan Ashcroft pads naked to the wall. He lifts the one lit torch, lights another and another and another until the darkness of their entire chamber is banished. His toned body seemingly glows with the soft orange flames.

Lastly, he chucks the torch in the wide-mouthed fireplace and the dry wood flares to life with a crackle and a pop. Their chamber maid had restocked it the other day. With the weather as warm as it's been, there hasn't been a need for the fire's warmth.

Amala says nothing to her husband during this task. Instead, she glares at him, knowing he has much to say on the matter, but he's refraining from doing so. Nothing irritates her more than unspoken words. He may be tired of having this argument, but she wishes, for once, he would believe her. Amala often wonders if he believes his daughter is Fate-blessed or if he thinks it's another 'story' his wife 'likes to tell.'

The queen knows he won't entertain the truth because the truth frightens him.

A fur robe is draped over the back of the hand-carved fireplace chair. It was given to him by his grandfather when he made it into the Onyx Guard. Thoughtfully, Davan touches the soft strands. He plucks it up, slides it across his shoulders, then strides to their chamber doors.

"Where are you going?" Amala hisses. She gathers herself onto her knees.

Davan pauses, shoulders pulled as though he's been struck against the spine. "The conversation is the same, Amala. First, we talk about the Divine. Then we worry over our daughter and her magic. Next, we worry about Sieba. Then you'll start to remind me how she's a puppet to Despair." He heaves a breath. "I won't entertain this any longer. I – I can't."

He reaches for the door handle and pulls it open. A chill wafts in from the unlit drafty castle halls, and when the door closes again, Amala climbs from her bed. She shuffles to the window and peers down at the houses. One by one, their torches are lit, brightening the streets as the workday begins.

If she can't convince her husband, then she'll have to take care of matters herself. She won't leave this alone until all safety measures are prepared to ensure her daughter's survival.

Chapter Three

The Shadled Forest is as quiet as always. No breeze stirs the plump purple leaves, nor does it rain to quench the cracked dirt the trunks' roots nestle into. It hardly rains in this forest, but when it does, the roots greedily drink and store the liquid in their leaves. That way, the trees can sip for days to come.

Nothing is guaranteed in the Shadled. Nothing should be expected of it either.

Just as it never rains, the sun can never penetrate the canopy of dark leaves. No plants grow on the forest floor as a result, and Queen Amala Ashcroft has always liked that the Shadled appears to be clean, neat, and tidy. Free of crunching leaves and brittle twigs. It makes for silent feet and deadly hunters.

This is the forest where the inexperienced and unprepared die. Only the toughest of beasts can survive here as there are no ponds for miles, and no rivers or lakes. And when someone stumbles across the nearest body of water, they run into the chance of being prey to a pyren. Pyrens are hypnotic swimming women with sharp teeth, tentacle hair, finned tails, and webbed fingers. They can swim in any form of liquid, including their realm's lava sea. Amala had heard stories about them as a child and always found them to be fascinating creatures.

Large glowing insects buzz from tree to tree, lighting up the darkness. The shadow people often collect the Diabolus Beetles and store them in lanterns. These are hung in the streets to minimize fire risk and next to children's beds to chase away the nightmares.

Amala used to help her mother with this task and had carried on the tradition with her own daughter.

Now, two lanterns are at the base of a trunk as Amala and her daughter, Princess Nefari dart from tree shadow to tree shadow. Here, in this deadly forest, a shadow person can truly be herself. For a royal child, it is a playground. It is a place where proper posture and formal words are abandoned in favor of screams of delight and giggling taunts.

As soon as one deep shadow swallows their dark forms, mother and daughter reappear in another. They play like this for at least an hour after scavenging for beetles, but they never travel far from their lanterns.

Shadow jumping is the shadow people's preferred method of traveling, and often, if the conditions are right and the individual is brave enough, they can travel far distances. It is risky to travel that far, for one simply does not know if they'll appear in a place with no shadows at all. Most shadow folk only travel to a shadow they can see in the distance. A shadow they're sure of.

"You can't get me, mama!" Nefari says cheerfully as she darts farther ahead. Every shadow surrounding them echoes it back, momentarily startling Amala. Usually, shadow whispering has to be taught, but Nefari has always been too smart for her own good. All it takes is for her to watch someone do something, and she understands how to accomplish it herself. She's never had to practice for much of anything, unlike Amala who had to gain her skills through extensive hard work. Bastian was as patient as ever, though.

Amala is grateful that this life – what they are – comes easy for Nefari. If only Amala knew Nefari's true gifts. Then, she could help her daughter harness them.

"I caught you last week! Today won't be any different!"

Nefari giggles adoringly. "Last week, I was seven!" She darts into a shadow and reappears from another shadow ten feet further.

Winded, Amala tips her head back and laughs as her bare feet fly across the forest floor. "You're still seven!" Nefari doesn't turn eight for a few more days. For reasons Amala can't fathom, her daughter believes the entire week is her birthday, and therefore, she is already eight.

"Nefari, slow down!" she adds half-heartedly. Nefari giggles again and disappears inside a shadow. The shadow ripples like poked water, wiggling with the little girl hiding, waiting, inside it.

"Silly girl," Amala coos. She slows before the shadow, hands on hips, and peers inside. Nefari thought she'd be clever, and her giggles echo once more through all the

26

forest's dark shadows. She thought her mother wouldn't see her from the angle where she slipped inside. But Amala was trained to hunt just like all the Shadow People. Sight isn't the only thing she hunts with.

Just before she follows her daughter inside, aiming to tickle until Nefari begs reprieve, her senses blare in alarm. It all but freezes her blood inside her sparkling black skin.

Nefari pops from a shadow with arms and fingers outstretched to tickle her mother. Amala leaps soundlessly and grabs her daughter around the waist. She claps a hand over the little girl's mouth and tugs her against the tree trunk, not daring to move, not daring to attempt a dash to the shadow's safety. The queen presses her spine into the jagged bark as her daughter stiffens in surprise. This isn't a game anymore.

"Shh," Amala shushes inside Nefari's slender ear.

The princess squeaks behind her mother's hand. Amala doesn't answer. Back the direction they came from, the glowing beetles wink out, one by one, hiding their light from the predatorial creature looming closer. Amala can feel its wrongness stretch over her skin.

"Mom?" Nefari mumbles against the palm, her child-like voice quivering. With every beetle's light distinguished, they're plunged into the darkness of the forest with no shadow to disappear into. They cannot shadow jump unless there's light to cast it. Complete darkness is impossible for them to maneuver in.

Quickly, Amala runs through the possible scenarios and escapes. Her white hair whips around with her frantic search. She looks to the plump purple leaves above. The creature is looming on the other side. She knows it, senses it. The wrongness thickens and the hair on her arms stand on end. Nefari wiggles, uncomfortable with the sensation that speaks of only dread.

"Wraiths," Amala breathes. Her heart pounds in her ears and against her ribs like a rabid prisoner banging against the bars in an empty, echoing dungeon. In the complete darkness, their starry skin gives away their location as well as a torch would. Wraiths are near impossible to outrun.

She can feel it getting closer, sense the ripe evil as it flies above the trees, circling for a way in. Amala could use her magic. She could produce a bright light to cast shadows and shove Nefari through, but she knows her daughter wouldn't go without her, and drawing that much attention to them will only double her chances of being ensnared by the wraith. That is if there's only one. There could be a pack of wraiths to contend with.

Frightened, but determined to calm her shaking daughter, Amala presses her lips to her daughter's white hair, closes her eyes, and hopes the wraiths will pass and the forest will light with its magic once more. Seconds tick by, and their hair starts to glow iridescent strands. She can see it behind her eyelids, and her pounding heart drops to her toes.

Amala curses.

Nefari screams behind Amala's hand, and her eyes fly open. The wraith, having caught the light, pushed through the purple leaves. Made of seemingly nothing but a foggy, misty black cloak, it soars in their direction. Amala spins

28

Nefari in her arms, picks her up, and darts through the darkness. She uses instinct alone to guide her between the trunks.

"Don't look!" Amala shouts to her. "Don't look, Nefari!"

Pressing her face into her mother's glittering black neck, Nefari wraps herself tightly around her mother. She starts to sob and tremble with fear.

Feet scraping against the dry cracked dirt, Amala runs as fast as she can toward the only place she knows there will be shadows to move through – the edge of the Shadled Forest. They're not far. They can't be. The Sea of Gold and its sharp blades of dazzling yellow grass is free from the trees' darkness. The sun always beats down on it, and the moon always provides enough light. *No matter the time of day, there will be shadows*, Amala rapidly thinks to herself.

In a moment of braveness, Nefari looks at the wraith chasing them through the trees. She can hear its ragged breaths, see it skeleton face with her sharp night vision. The creature is cloaked in black smoke that doesn't whisp the way it should. Traveling at this speed, cloth would be dangling behind, whipped around by the breeze of momentum. Instead, the smoky tendrils curl and sway, undisturbed by the speed in which they travel.

"Mommy, hurry!" Nefari screams.

There, just ahead, the forest's thick trunks open to a field of gold grass. Amala nearly sobs. Her throat feels hoarse from her ragged breath, and she swallows to no relief while pushing her body to the limit.

29

The Sea of Gold is named by the centaurs whose white-capped mountains push to the sky at the other end of the field. The mountains are dotted with young and old pine trees and fat blobs of snow ready to tumble down the steep slopes at a slight disturbance. If so, it would come to its final rest at the Sea of Gold.

The blades of grass are as gold as the name suggests, and they glisten in the large moon's light like hundreds of fancy knives under the scrutiny of torch-light.

A sob of relief wracks Amala's body, and she plunges forward, weaving between trunks. Her arms grip her daughter more tightly, and she stops at the edge of the forest.

The queen glances up at the moon. It's barely night, the short time of the evening where the moon isn't bright enough to cast deep enough shadows. *Unless…* she searches wildly, sweat stinging at her pores. She'll have to run along the grass and follow the line of trees until there's a shadow.

"He's coming!" Nefari screams. Her nails dig into her mother's shoulders. Amala hardly notices the sharp pain nor the slick feeling of the welling blood.

Amala looks behind her, and gritting her teeth, she places her dark bare foot on the gold grass. Immediately, the grass slices into her feet, demanding blood for the crossing. The Sea of Gold is not nourished from water. It is blood that feeds it. The only ones not affected by it are the creatures with hooves.

Most things on this realm demand one thing or another. An eye for an eye. A sacrifice for a sacrifice. Amala had anticipated this, would have dreaded it if her life wasn't in danger – if her daughter's life wasn't in danger. Bastian had made her step onto the sharp razors over and over again when she was fifteen. By the end of her fifteenth year, she had built up a small tolerance to the pain of the tiny slices. This time will be different. Before, she didn't have her daughter's added weight to contend with. The cuts will be deeper, more severe.

Gritting her teeth, she plunges in and screams in pain.

"Move, mommy! Please! Please, run!"

The wraith roars, and adrenaline surges inside the queen. The wraith is here for Nefari; Amala is sure of it.

Over the years, Amala had heard the rumors from the Kingdom of Salix. Suspicions from travelers and traders mostly, but it was confirmed when Amala secretly helped nurse a crone back to health in exchange for information. Fate hadn't told her much before he merged his magic with her daughter's, and she wanted to know more of what might be in store for the future.

Regarding the crone, Amala didn't learn much more than she already knew, but she did glean two things: Queen Seiba wants her daughter, the Fate-blessed Princess of Shadows, and Queen Sieba is possessed by Despair. Amala has no doubt in her mind that Despair is behind the wraiths. It takes great magic to produce them, and who better than a god who needs assassins to hunt the last remaining remnants of Fate?

We have to get home, Amala chants to herself, urging her legs to move faster and faster despite the agony. Only then can they travel to the safety of their castle where this creature won't be able to enter. The Shadow Kingdom exists within a shadow within the Divine Realm itself. It's impossible to find unless the seeker knows the way. It took Amala years to learn how to punch through the creep and find the kingdom. A wraith isn't smart enough to do the same.

There! Amala's blood thrums with relief. Just ahead, the Sea of Gold pushes into the forest, forcing the tree's line to curve. At this angle to the moon, shadows sprawl across the grass. Amala's muscles scream, but she thunders forward, closer and closer. *Almost there.*

The queen trips over an exposed root, and Nefari screams as they tumble. Amala turns her body so her back lands against the slicing blades, leaving her daughter unharmed. It feels like sharp needles as the grass cuts into her back, along her arms, and through her thin dress. The queen's eyes prick with tears, and she blinks blearily at the wraith racing toward its prey.

Heart in throat, Amala raises a hand, and a beam of light shoots from her palm. It sounds like air pushing through a cannon, and it lightens the night further as it soars in an arch.

The wraith weaves in the air, missing the light, but it's enough to slow the creature down. It's enough for Amala to gather her feet back under her and race for the shadows once more with Nefari in her arms. Her feet are slick with her own blood, but she leaps into the air, diving for the shadows. They swallow the two of them, and carry her and her daughter to safety.

Chapter Four

Amala and Nefari land with a thud on the blue, purple, and green cobbled streets of the Shadow Kingdom. The street eventually leads to the small castle, but from here, it can't be seen over the shops with straw-covered roofs. This particular street weaves a path between the shops, branching into other streets that steer the shadow people to their homes.

Nefari's sobs are loud as she climbs off her mother's stomach, gathers herself to her feet, and wraps her arms around her middle. She glances around at the shops, lanterns dark for the night.

Groaning and shaking, Amala rises. Her dress is torn, and her bleeding feet leave prints on the stone. Davan isn't going to like this. She looks back to the creep, the darkness they pushed through to enter the kingdom. She feels uncertain, still endures the lingering evil of the wraith. She squints at the velvety darkness that seems to roll in on itself, ears straining.

A shop bell rings, and the two royals glance at the opening door.

"Go home, Nefari," Amala urges her daughter softly, eyeing the man and woman now staring at them. "Go. Find a healer. I'll be there shortly." Nefari doesn't move.

"My Queen?" Hoyt Riversdale asks as he steps instinctively toward them. Age has wrinkled the skin around his eyes wide with shock. Rolls of silk are bundled in his bulky arms, and he adjusts their awkward position. Amala can just see the bridge of his hawkish nose above his burden.

His wife, Gen, closes her shop door distractedly, tugging it absentmindedly at her back. She's round around the belly, plump in the face, and her dry and wild white hair is pinned at the nape of her neck. The shop bell rings again, but this time, it's distant, echoing inside the enclosed space.

Amala and Nefari must appear worse for wear because Gen Riversdale's expression is anything but calm. "My Divine," she curses. Her hand hovers near her mouth, and her eyes bulge. Both husband and wife are in their human form. Here, in the darkness and safety of their home, it is common for shadow people to prefer this form, but Amala can tell Gen is contemplating on switching to her shadow form. She can sense the danger.

Hoyt pays no mind to his wife. He lowers the rolls of blue and white silk to the stones near the shop's door. "What is it?" he asks as he rights himself. He moves slowly as if not to frighten the two royals more than they already appear.

"Hoyt," Amala breathes. Her feet and back ache, and she shifts her stance to relieve the pressure of both her dress pressing against wounds and the stones jabbing into sore feet. His keen eyes narrow at the bloody prints then squint further at Nefari's tears.

Amala bends to her stubborn daughter, wiping the hair from her face. They're both still in their shadow forms, and Nefari's tears reflect the starry skin, making each speck they roll over appear as tiny diamonds. "Are you hurt?"

"No, momma."

Sighing with relief, Amala kisses her daughter's forehead.

"What happened?" Hoyt barks.

"Please escort Nefari to the castle." Amala tries to keep her voice from shaking but fails. She stands full once more, a supportive hand on the back of her daughter's shoulder. He would have seen right through her bravado anyway.

Amala has known Hoyt since she was Nefari's age. No. No, before then, too, though she doesn't remember anything from her infant and toddler years. Most children don't.

Anointed by her father, Hoyt Riversdale is Captain to the Onyx Guard. An honorable man hell-bent on truth-telling and speaking his mind. Her father and Hoyt were good friends for this very reason.

Being a part of the Onyx Guard is usually a family obligation, passed down from father to son or daughter. The Riversdale family is no exception. They've protected and served the shadow royals as far back as the kingdom's records go. Sometimes, Amala has wondered how much deeper their loyalty goes than normal citizens of the Shadow Kingdom.

The moon-shaped scar that curves around the right hand's middle finger's knuckle seems almost fated to her. Fated to serve. Fated to be loyal. Fated for duty. This is the mark of the Onyx Guard.

Nefari has always been fascinated with Hoyt's son Vale and the moon-shaped scar already visible on his knuckle. Both children are of the same age and have been close friends since birth. Now that they're getting older, both Amala and Hoyt have seen something deeper blossom between the two. Something that makes both of them blush when they peek at each other when they think the other isn't aware. It's endearing and reminds Amala that love is both pure and innocent, two things that can be taken from an individual so swiftly.

"What is it? What's wrong?" Hoyt is in front of Amala now. He settles a hand on her shoulder, urging her to speak.

"There was a wraith," Nefari says. Her tears have stopped flowing, and she angrily swipes at her runny nose with the back of her hand.

Amala inhales, waiting for Hoyt's lecture on the dangers of traveling to the Shadled without proper protection. "A wraith found us in the Shadled –"

Hoyt's eyes darken, and he glances at his wife who's slowly approaching. "Take Nefari to King Davan. Do as the queen says, and find her a healer. Have another waiting for the queen."

Obediently, his wife nods. Amala gently pushes Nefari in her direction. "Go, little one. I'll follow you shortly."

Swallowing thickly, Nefari tightens her lips as tears twinkle in her eyes once more. Gen Riversdale wraps an arm around Nefari's small shoulders, shushing to her softly, and together, they rush down the quiet street.

Hoyt watches her go. His instincts tell him something is wrong. Something is off. Heart waging between honor and love, he fights the urge to escort his wife to the castle for fear that she may be ensnared into whatever this bad feeling will result in.

Most of the shadow people are in their homes for the evening. With the exception of the fabric shop, the shops closed over an hour ago. Gen had stayed open longer to make the royal garments for Nefari's birthday ball tomorrow night. She has taken extra care to stitch each dress and tunic with perfection, honored that she was tasked with such a duty. As a result, she's been spending long hours at the shop, worrying over choices in colors and traditional hemming.

When Hoyt was finished with his duties for the evening, he had sought out his wife so they could spend time together before being bombarded by their children. As often as they dare, they find time to make their way home together.

Just minutes ago, they had been grinning at each other over a private joke, then kissed passionately under the shop's lantern. Now, this imposing dread is chasing away the quiet moment they had shared between the two of them.

As the last echoes of their feet fade, Hoyt turns his attention back to the queen. "You've always been a bit reckless, but never with Nefari's safety."

A muscle in Amala's cheek feathers. She's used to Hoyt chastising her, but he has to know this was never her intention. All she wanted was to provide memories for her daughter like Amala's mother did for her.

Since her father died nine years ago, Hoyt has attempted to 'slip on the shoes' a father would normally fill. Amala adores Hoyt. She trusts him with her whole heart, but she doesn't like the way he sees her. She can tell the Captain of the Onyx Guard still thinks she's the little girl who got stuck climbing a Shadled tree and needed his help to get her back down.

He and Iseal were great friends, and Amala has often thought of Hoyt as an uncle instead of a guardian. Amala wets her lips. It's time he starts seeing her for what she is: his queen.

"We haven't seen the wraiths in quite some time," she growls back defensively. "I thought it safe!"

"They're assassins, Amala. They don't run on anyone's timeframe but theirs and the Queen of Salix's."

You mean Despair's. She tugs on the roots of her hair. "Don't you think I know that?"

"Sometimes I wonder."

Dropping her hands back to her sides, she sighs. "I hadn't sensed any danger. I let my guard down, and for that, I'll take the fault."

He's silent as he studies her, weighing his next words and if they're a necessary. "You should have taken an escort. Any one of the Guard would have been happy to –" He pauses, glancing over her shoulder to the creep. His expression furrows as he studies it.

"Hoyt?" Amala frowns and follows his line of sight when he doesn't immediately respond. Then, she slowly turns her body. There, traveling through it, is the wraith who had chased them. The black foggy cloak detaches from the darkness and the creature enters the cobbled street.

"No," Amala whispers. She backs a step, bumping straight into Hoyt's chest. This is what she's been fearing. This is what her husband promised would never happen. The creep is promised to be impenetrable by those who don't know how to enter. How? How did the wraith . . .

Amala gulps and bumps her back against Hoyt once more, forgetting he was standing there. The wraith had watched them disappear into the shadow and, somehow, had learned to do it too.

Every instinct inside her tells her to flee. These creatures leave destruction wherever they go. They can possess. They can destroy. They will kill. They're assassins.

"Run," Hoyt whispers, his voice dazed. He stirs to action, grabs her shoulders, and shoves her aside. The whine of his sword being pulled from its sheath disrupts the ominous quiet. "Run, Amala!"

She looks at the sword, then the wraith. The wraith seems to grow in size while it leisurely surveys the kingdom, hungry and full of obvious anticipation. A sword won't do anything against this creature of dark magic. Only magic can beat magic.

Gritting her teeth, Amala gathers the light in herself, her star-flecked form brightening. The magic thrums as it builds and builds inside her chest, running down her arms like a cold wash. She squares her stance, preparing herself. Magic is always hard on her body like it was never meant to be there in the first place, but somehow, the shadow royals acquired it. Survival? Evolution? Fate's insurance? Amala has never truly known.

"Amala!" Hoyt shouts at her then shoves her aside as the wraith dives for the two of them. Amala blasts her magic at the wraith, and the light punches straight through the wisps of its cloak.

The creature tips his head back and screams a thousand screams. Amala and Hoyt drop to their knees, hands over their sensitive ears. Hoyt's body flickers back and forth between human and shadow form as if the onslaught of sound is too much for his body to endure.

With a thunderclap, the wraith is gone. The two slowly lower their hands, gazing at where the wraith once floated. Little specks of the wispy black cloak float down like feathers until they rest against the cobbled streets. The silence feels deafening, and the atmosphere feels void without the clinging sensation of despair.

Amala follows a piece of wispy cloak and watches it settle onto a blue stone. It evaporates like steam as if the wraith itself was made from nothing but wet air.

Magic. Dark magic. That's what they're made from.

41

"She knows," Amala whispers. She raises her gaze to the darkness beyond. "Queen Sieba knows." *Despair has found us.*

Chapter Five

"If she didn't know how to enter our kingdom before, she does now," Hoyt says. His tone has a bitter edge.

Amala looks at him, watching as he scrubs his jaw. "Why don't you ever listen? You should have retreated to the safety of the castle, as I asked."

Amala snorts and stands to full height. "You could not have killed that wraith by yourself. Only royals have magic, Hoyt. It takes magic to kill that sort of creature. A creature whose purpose today was to find the Shadow Kingdom or destroy my daughter." Amala blinks, then snarls, "Both probably. They're -"

"Minions of Queen Sieba, I know." He crosses his arms. "If it was so easy to take one down here, why didn't you kill it in the Shadled? It would have never traveled here if it was dead. Sieba's magic —"

"It's Despair's magic," Amala barks at him. Someone has to believe her. Someone has to believe her that the Queen of Salix is corrupt by Despair's hand. "And I didn't want to risk it. I didn't know if there were more of them in the Shadled, and I didn't want to risk Nefari being taken."

43

Hoyt is quiet for a long moment, studying the face of the woman he's considered a daughter for her whole life. "King Davan will not be happy about this."

Amala snorts again. "My husband isn't happy about a lot of things these days." She begins a brisk walk toward the castle, refusing to show weakness by wincing at the pain in her feet. Hoyt matches her step for step. "It will be nothing new."

"He has a lot of stress with the threat of Queen Sieba."

They come to a fork in the road and pause. The middle road leads to the courtyard that squats around half of the castle. The outer two curve and river between houses similarly styled to the shops.

The Diabolus Beetle lanterns are bright in some of the home's windows. Every second another fat beam of light splashes across the road in rectangular gold silhouettes. The wraith's death was loud. Now the curious villagers are awakening and the night has only begun. Amala almost curses under her breath. She was hoping to be able to talk with her husband before anyone else would question the misfortunes of this evening.

In the background, she can hear the displeased whinnying of the horses in the stables and the baying cries of sheep scattered in confining pens behind homes. No doubt they sensed the dark evil of the wraith and have been causing a ruckus ever since.

An Onyx Guard, pale in his human form, jogs down the street and approaches the two. He's tall for his youth, a boy stretching into a man, and his limbs are gangly and

44

awkward on him. Despite his build, he looks just like his father.

"Iger," Amala greets warily.

From the direction he came, he must have been at home. Did the noise of the wraith's death wake him, too, or was he already patrolling the streets?

Amala gets a whiff of him then examines his hands caked with grime. The royal stables then, tending to the horses. Amala wonders what he did to deserve a task usually reserved for horse master apprentices.

"My Queen," Iger Riversdale says, breathless. He dips his head in respect to Amala, then nods to Hoyt. "Sir."

"Iger, if you call me sir one more time, I'm going to smack the side of your head, then tell that gal – what's her name?"

"Beau," Amala supplies, slightly annoyed for the interruption. She glances at the castle, barely in view. Beau is her lady, a servant who's specifically for Amala alone, and one of Amala's trusted friends.

"That's right, Beau. I'm going to tell her that you call her name in your dreams."

Iger grins at his father but ignores his idle threats. The worry is still in his eyes, and it has nothing to do with his current teenage fascination. "We heard a –"

"Yes, yes," Hoyt says, waving his hand impatiently. He quickly recounts everything that had just happened. Amala watches as the tension increases in the boy's posture. She flicks a glance behind him, wondering if this is how everyone will behave with the news or if she should expect worse.

Iger's face pales visibly. He gapes past his father's shoulder, searching. "Are there more?"

"No." Hoyt leers accusingly at Amala. "Just the one, and the queen has taken care of it. Alert the Onyx Guard. Let the kingdom know before the rumors begin. The last thing we need is hysteria."

Amala nods, grateful he didn't lie to Iger. Honesty has always been her promise to her people. She refuses to start lying now, no matter how scary the circumstance was, is, and will be.

Iger nods, turns on his heel, and jogs to the villagers cautiously exiting their homes.

Amala turns to Hoyt. "This could end badly," he says without looking at her.

"If someone would have heeded my warnings from the beginning, we wouldn't be in this mess."

"Are you referring to your husband or me?"

Amala shrugs, unable to hide her wince this time, and begins back toward the castle. "Both."

"At the time, there was nothing to take seriously."

"You cannot honestly believe that," Amala taunts. She has the urge to kick a stray stone but refrains. It wouldn't be queenly. "A wraith got in, Hoyt. I've been telling you this might happen for years. That we can't count on the creep as our sole means of protection when it comes to Queen Sieba and Despair. Despair is darkness, you fool.

46

Darkness! What do you think the darkness will do to the shadow people? Hmm?"

He purses his lips and slides his hands into his pockets, thoughtfully peering up at the castle. All the lanterns and torches must be lit, because every window is as bright as the village houses have become. It enhances the courtyard with splashes of buttery yellow across the stone paths and the iridescent garden full of purple, blue, and pink flowers. Black shimmering vines crawl across a portion of the courtyard, stretching and weaving until they reach the castle. From there, they latch and wind around the bricks, creating a leaf's equivalent to a waterfall. It's as though the vines themselves are what's keeping the sturdy castle upright, a stunning sight to be sure.

"That has never been done," he mutters. His tone is thoughtful instead of angry and defensive, and it makes Amala sigh. "Why would anyone think differently? Why would they assume the barrier that once kept us safe would no longer continue to do so?"

"But," Hoyt grabs the queen's arm gently and pulls her to a stop. "Just because the wraith made it through doesn't mean others will be able to. It was an accident. An unfortunate coincidence. For it to happen again is extremely unlikely."

"That's not good enough," Amala growls. "It's an excuse to do nothing. To pretend that the world isn't changing around you. To convince yourself that Fate was wrong and that his sacrifice to my daughter was just a precaution instead of an omen." Amala snarls in his face. "You're scared. That is why you refuse to believe what your own eyes see."

47

A servant bustles past the two, and Amala straightens her torn and bloody dress. The woman says nothing, but she regards them curiously, making sure Hoyt sees her glare is directed at him and him alone. Hoyt pretends he's unaware of the woman, but Amala knows better. He would have retorted by now, otherwise.

All the castle servants are there by choice, and all of them adore Amala. She treats them like friends instead of the help, and in this moment, she's grateful to have at least one person on her side, even if that person has no idea why Amala needs defending. *She will soon, though,* Amala thinks as the woman bustles past the last row of flowers and disappears under the white blossoming dwarf tree.

"Fine," Hoyt says reluctantly. "I'll send a few men to guard the Shadled tonight and alert us to any more trouble stirring inside them. If there is something to worry about, they'll alert us."

The sound of a crashing wave fills the courtyard, and King Davan shirks from the shadows, clad in his shadow form. Amala can feel his emotions churn inside him and fights the urge to meet his rage head-on. She's had enough of all the testosterone posturing today.

Davan's black sparkling skin lightens into pale pink flesh as he approaches his queen. The bottom of his cloak hovers above the stones, and under its velvety cloth, Amala spies the leather straps of his training gear. He had come straight from sparring, and a pang of guilt surges inside Amala. The guilt makes her feel naked, exposed, prickling her insides. She struggles to squash it.

"Amala!" he cries gratefully. Two Onyx Guards lumber from the shadow he had just emerged from. Their attention swivels and assesses while Amala's own strays to Hoyt with blame sparking in her bold gaze.

Davan opens his arms as he rushes to Amala. His leather shoes are soundless in tread, formed perfectly to the curves of his feet. The black smokey crown on his head jerks like a flame. He folds her into his arms, and she returns the embrace as his warmth seeps into the chill that's crept across her skin.

"Gen told me there was danger," he says in her ear. "Nefari is with a healer! When I didn't find you near the shops, I started to panic. What happened?" His fingers are firm as he grips her shoulders, pulling away to study every inch of her face. Feeling safe surrounded by the Onyx Guard, Amala's skin fades into the same shade her husband now wears. Her wounds look more severe in this form, and Davan hisses at the evidence.

"There was a wraith," Amala grumbles. She scratches the back of her neck nervously, revealing her ruined clothes. Although she can't help the nervous gesture, her voice is tinged with anger, and she directs that anger toward her husband.

In her mind, this is his fault. He did not listen to her. Perhaps she should have never allowed him to make all the decisions on this matter in the first place. She should have gone with her gut and taken all the precautions years ago. For that, she is to blame.

The royal couple stares at one another and an uncomfortable silence settles between the Onyx Guards.

One of them should have been with her, and just as Amala is blaming her husband, Hoyt is blaming the two men guarding Davan's back. He is captain, after all. They all have their orders, and today, everyone failed.

"Where?" Davan finally growls. The crown pulses.

"In the Shadled, sir," Hoyt says. His spine snaps to attention. Amala glances at him and hardly suppresses a snarl when she sees the respect he's giving her husband. He refuses to show the same respect to her. Her father and mother would turn in their graves if they could see the kingdom now.

The power lies within the shadow queen. When her mother died, it was up to her father to take her place, and the kingdom grew too comfortable with a male ruler.

Amala grinds her teeth. She should have corrected this misjudgment as soon as she became queen, but alas, she had more important things to deal with than who their subjects listened to more. If she couldn't get her husband to heed her warning, then how was she to gain the respect of her people? Perhaps now that all her warnings are directly in front of him, he'll step aside with his stubborn resolve and allow her to take the lead.

Davan visibly relaxes with relief, and her hope dashes. "Thank the Divine," he says, as though everything has been returned to normal. This wasn't the reaction she had dared to anticipate.

"No," Amala growls. "We can't thank them. Fate is dead. Prayers to both Choice and Hope go unanswered. They are nowhere to be found. And the last remaining Divine is ruling the eastern continent. Despair is puppeting the Queen of Salix. She's abducting free people for slavery, dealing with the dark arts, and pushing the boundaries of her rule. She sent the wraith, Davan. She will continue to send them until she can find a weakness in our defenses. Until she has Nefari, dead or alive. Until Despair is satisfied."

"Not this again, Amala," Davan says through clenched teeth. He steps away as though her assumed madness is contagious. His cheeks redden with rage or embarrassment, Amala isn't sure, but she feels a pang of hurt anyway.

Amala invades the space he just vacated. "The wraith punched through the creep on its own."

A muscle quivers in Davan's cheek as he stares down at his wife. His gaze moves behind her to the darkness that makes the edge of their kingdom, then to Hoyt.

"Is this true?" he asks. Hoyt nods in confirmation. "How?"

"I don't know." Amala holds out her bloody hand, pleading. The gesture, and her tone, beg her husband to direct his questions to her and her alone. "I don't know, but . . ."

Hoyt and the two Onyx Guards look down at their feet, shame paling the already creamy parlor of their faces. She doesn't have to say more. Every single shadow person will understand what it means that the wraiths had broken their largest method of defense. Queen Sieba Arsonian now knows where the kingdom is located, where Nefari lives, and now, she can enter. Her wraiths can enter. Her army can enter.

"It was only a matter of time. . ." Amala whispers, and her husband's shadow crown flares once more. He looks away, shame blossoming red patches on his cheeks like a budding rose in the morning's sun.

The five of them are quiet as they wait for the news to fully settle, but it never does. Instead, the implications of what's to come leech away every strain of hope they once had for the Shadow Kingdom's continued safety.

A single tear beads at the corner of Amala's eye. She blinks, and it dribbles down her chilled skin to the edge of her jaw. It lingers there, cold and dreary.

"Orders, sir?" Hoyt whispers when the silence becomes weighted with a sense of foreboding.

Amala stares into the eyes of her husband beseechingly. Actions must be taken. Precautions must be attempted. The queen's gaze moves to the patches of flowers where her mother used to read to her. She studies the bench Hoyt had added for Amala and her daughter to continue the tradition. Above them, the castle's windows wink with flashing firelight, and inside one on the second floor, in a room where Amala's heart truly lies, her daughter peers down at them. Once spotted, Nefari flees back into her room.

Davan turns and begins to head toward the castle. He shifts into his shadow form, and his cloak whips behind his brisk pace.

"Sir?" Hoyt plods forward and then blinks at the loudness of his voice.

Davan stops and looks sidelong over his shoulder. "My wife began this. She can see it through."

Another tear spills from her cheek. When had Davan and Amala become so distant? They were once so in love. Her father had boasted about the good match even from his deathbed. But tonight . . .

Tonight, he dismissed, accepted, and blamed her all in two sentences. Amala never thought it would hurt so much to feel all three things. He let her go. He accepted her as queen. He blames her for the wraith. And now he's walking away from her.

"He's turned his back on me," she whispers to nobody. The only person left is Hoyt, and Amala can hear his thick swallow. She can tell he doesn't know what to say.

"You're sure about all this?" Hoyt asks, a gentle change of subject. "You're sure the Queen of Salix will come for the kingdom?"

The queen's fingers curl into fists and she sucks in a deep breath, refusing to shed another tear. "I'll lay down my life for my daughter and this kingdom. If I wasn't sure, I wouldn't have said anything years ago. Fate had told me what was coming. He told me, Hoyt." Amala turns to face him, refusing to admit her secret: that a crone had filled in the blanks.

"Okay," he whispers, staring down at her with a sense of trust.

"I need you to do me a favor."

He blinks, unsurprised.

She peeks around, making sure no one else is listening. "I need you to make sure the crones and the centaurs are coming to tomorrow's birthday ball."

"Why?"

Amala rolls her shoulders, breathes deep, and wills her shadow crown to appear on her head. "One of the leaders owes me a favor, and the other is a dear friend."

"Their attendance has already been confirmed. Attending the princess's ball won't be suspicious to your people, Amala, but holding a secret meeting with them certainly will. You can't just leave the party and -"

"The meeting won't take place during the ball. I'd like to meet with them beforehand. In the morning preferably. After the hunters return."

"Where shall I ask them to convene with you?" he asks slowly.

Amala grins, a sly spread of her lips. "In the Shadled, of course."

Davan won't like that she snuck to the forest a day after the wraith attack, but the situation calls for risks.

Chapter Six

The king sighs in his seat as the Shadow Kingdom's council convenes around the oblong black table. Bowls of freshly peeled citrus fruits march down the middle. They fill the immediate space with their sour scents, an aroma Davan can't help but love.

Popular across the kingdoms, these fruits are harvested in villages within Urbana's borders. Davan imagines they cost a fortune, but then again, the continent of Urbana's wealth lies with slave trade, not fruits. They shouldn't be expensive when the labor is free.

Sometimes, it disgusts Davan that Shadled Forest sprawls across a portion of Urbana. He wants no part in the slave trade, and by trading with them, he feels like he's playing a part in it.

This particular shipment was traded with Diabolus Beetle, the bright toxic beetles that frolic through the Shadled Forest. Normally deadly, if diluted, it can be used as a drug. Urbana's rich pay handsomely for it, and if Amala ever found out about the trade, she'd never talk to him again. Trading their prized wool isn't enough to keep the kingdom fed these days. The Shadled won't grow crops, and the people can't only consume the game they hunt.

Meetings like this occur only in the throne room where servants bring in the chairs, assemble the table, and linger to provide refreshments. Pressing his tongue to the inside of his cheek, Davan wishes they could meet somewhere else because he swears he can feel the thrones stare down at him disapprovingly. He feels like a failure, an impostor, and today is not any different.

A wraith. A wraith had made it through the creep. And his behavior … Davan fights the urge to growl at his own thoughts.

When he and Amala were matched, he had not thought the responsibilities would feel so heavy. He hadn't known that every time his people felt fear, his insides would scream in terror. He hadn't known that his dreams would be plagued with dread for their future, or worries over the smallest details that may never become validated. His responsibilities have made him exhausted, and tonight, he was more than happy to hand it all back to his wife.

Having been pulled from their beds, some of the council members are still dressed in their night clothes, white hair haphazard from sleep. They needed to be told of the truths before the lies could spread and taint the kingdom. He had listened, impatiently tapping his foot, to the priest's opening prayer as he beseeched Fate to bless them, a Divine who no longer exists. He had nodded at his sister's concerns over what a lock-down could mean for the trade. He had bit his tongue, tasting blood, when their General suggested immediate retaliation on Salix, a completely implausible action. They have no ships to cross Widow's Bay. They don't have enough horses for an army to outrun the terrors within the Frozen Fades. Nor can they shadow jump to an empire none have ever been to.

They're scared, but no more scared than a father whose daughter is in more danger now than she ever has been. And then his wife who he had. . . *oh Divine, his wife.* He fights the urge to thump his head against the table.

The conversation eventually carried on without him, and he allowed his mind to drift. All he can think about is his actions an hour earlier. The actions and unspoken words between him and his wife were less than savory. They were childish.

He shunned her. He turned his back on her. He's never done that. Not so blatantly, directly, and publicly. Sure, he'll disapprove of what she will say or do, for she is spontaneous and wild, but this feels different. The king has never gone so far to hurt his wife simply because the fear inside him is too strong for him to bear alone.

"My King?" a gentle woman calls to him from down the table. Davan blinks. Everyone is staring at him, watching his unseeing eyes as he had gazed at nothing in particular. His sister grins knowingly at him then coughs to cover an abrupt chuckle.

He sits up straighter. "Apologies. Can you repeat that?" At this moment, a servant sneaks forward and tops off his already full goblet, mistaking the clearing of his throat as a need for more beverage. Davan thanks the servant and gulps a few swallows of the red bitter wine. The servant bows and backs away.

The woman, old enough to be his mother, looks around nervously. She pulls on the ends of her bent and aged fingers, pinching the brittle nails. "Should we call off the princess's birthday ball? Because of the threat?" she adds when Davan appears taken aback by such a suggestion.

"They're worried about our foreign guests, sir," Hoyt whispers helpfully. He had leaned forward to speak in the King's ear, and it had startled him. Davan had forgotten Hoyt was standing directly behind him. He looks to him now, pursing his lips to hide the fact that twice now, he's been caught unawares.

Since leaving Amala in the care of the healer, the captain of the Onyx Guard has been oddly quiet. He had slipped in last minute, seeming flustered and pale-faced. Davan is surprised Hoyt had heard a word of the debate at all, for he, too, seemed to be lost in his own thoughts. Perhaps he's better at multitasking. This has always been Davan's downfall. He can only focus on one thing at a time, and everything else melts away like fresh butter on hot baked bread.

"No," Davan says, turning back to the council. "Let our guests come. If anything, the centaurs and other royals will further aid us if they discover us in need of protection."

"Are we expecting an attack?" the priest asks.

"No. Right now, we have no reason to believe the Queen of Salix will attack."

"It would take her weeks to prepare her army and cross Widow's Bay," the general chimes in. He bites into a yellow fruit in a self-satisfied sort of way. From where Davan sits,

58

he can hear the slosh of his teeth cutting through juices. "The presence of the centaurs will put the people at ease."

Amala would never forgive him if he turned the centaurs away without providing hospitality, especially since they're making the journey down from the Kadoka Mountains. It is not often they'll leave the safety of their peaks and snow. Amala adores them, and therefore, so does Nefari. He's already disappointed his wife today. He won't do the same for his daughter.

"And the crones?" the older woman asks.

"Allow them to come as well."

"But, My King-" she blubbers.

Davan holds up a hand. Her name finally dawns on him. "I know about the crone's, Lace. They're Despair's creations. They're cunning liars. They're sadistic." Davan leans forward in his chair and steeples his fingers. He's surprised to find the tips slightly numb with cold. "My wife has asked them here. Your queen. She will not cower in the face of Despair, and neither should you. They'll come, and they'll receive the same hospitality as the centaurs. No further discussion will be had concerning their attendance, or any of the others, royals included."

He meets each of their eyes until they nod. The meeting is quick to adjourn after that. Any further questions about security measures to be taken, Davan advises the council to direct them to Amala. She can handle that part. She was trained to manage such matters since birth. In fact, he's sure she would appreciate being included, and hopefully, this can be the gesture that begins his apology.

As the council files out of the throne room, Davan remains in his seat. He dismisses the servants, who leave the clay jugs of wine. His personal servant lightly sets his own jug next to the king's elbow, and Davan thanks him for his thoughtfulness and foresight.

The general is the last of the council to leave, reluctantly Davan notes, but Hoyt lingers. Davan can feel him brimming with questions, and with a wave of his hand, he gestures for the Captain of the Onyx Guard to sit. He likes to think of them as friends, but Hoyt refuses to give up using Davan's title. Rank is something the man understands. Davan appreciates it, but in a castle full of servants and bowing and scraping, he sometimes wishes someone would see the man underneath the crown.

"Is Amala with Nefari?"

"She should be," Hoyt says quietly. "That's where she said she was going next, after the healer." Davan pours him wine, and Hoyt sneers at it skeptically before sighing, grabbing the goblet, and guzzling the red liquid. Slowly, carefully, he sets the goblet back on the table. He runs his finger over the gold rim, gathering wetness.

"Speak, Hoyt. I cannot bear your silent questions."

He flicks his gaze to the king, peering at him from under long white lashes. "The eighth birthday of a Royal Shadow is typically when their magic arises."

Davan rolls his shoulders. Born without a drop of royal blood in him, Davan has never had magic. He has never known what it feels like to wield it, and rarely has he watched his wife use her own.

Amala's magic consists of light and heat. On Amala's mother's 8th birthday, a second shadow appeared. This second shadow could move freely and come in handy on more than one occasion. Amala's grandmother could manipulate sounds, and the list goes on from there. Somewhere in this castle, an entire book is dedicated to the royal's magical history. Davan had only glanced at it once, around the time Amala told him she was with child. It scared him enough that he hadn't read too far in.

The married couple has often discussed what Nefari's magic might be, and with Fate's essence inside her, it may affect their daughter in ways they cannot foresee. While the future of their daughter is Amala's favorite subject, it is Davan's least. He doesn't like uncertainties.

He rubs his hands over his face, attempting to scrub away the stress settled heavily under his eyes. "What about it?"

"Has there been any signs of her power?"

"No. Why do you ask?" Davan tips his head to the side. Everyone knows the magic appears on the eighth birthday to the exact second of when the child was born. No other signs would appear beforehand.

Enlightenment stretches across the king's face, and his lips twist in a snarl. He refrains from thumping his fist against the table. "My daughter will not be asked to protect the kingdom from whatever may be coming our way. It takes years to master magic, Hoyt. Years. Asking a child to defend her kingdom before she can properly learn to defend herself is absurd. And," he leans forward, "it could kill her. Using too much magic could kill her, especially when she's not ready for it."

"But she has Fate's-"

He slices an arm through the air angrily. "That means nothing. We do not know what Fate's blessing has in store for my daughter. We don't know when it will appear, in what form, or if it ever will. And we aren't going to test it."

Hoyt looks away, embarrassed for bringing up the subject.

Taking a calming breath, Davan slumps back in his chair. "Is Vale prepared for tomorrow?"

"He is," Hoyt nods stiffly.

"Good. Good."

"Are we continuing with the announcement?"

"Yes." Davan's eyes snap to the Captain. "The people could use some happy news. Announcing Vale and Nefari's future marriage will raise everyone's spirits." Davan smirks. Though the special day is ten years away, Davan has dreamed of it since the moment he first held her.

"Nefari has had no complaints about the match, either," Davan continues distractedly. "I believe she has taken quite the liking to your son."

"Vale has been agreeable to the match as well." Hoyt stands, satisfied with this answer. He straightens his tunic, snapping the hem to free the wrinkles. "I'll see you tomorrow evening, My King."

Davan nods to him, grabs the vase, and pours himself more wine. The children have been more than agreeable to the match. What was once a playful routine of running through the castle and chasing each other from one end to the other has turned into flirtatious giggles and pinches. His little girl will someday not be his little girl anymore, and tomorrow feels like a nail in that coffin of inevitable truth.

Groaning, Davan gulps his wine.

Chapter Seven

In the quiet of the princess's room, Amala stands behind her daughter, who sits cross-legged on a stool in front of her vanity. Slowly, Amala brushes her fine strands of white hair in chunks at a time, mesmerized by how something so solid can feel so liquid. Her servant, Beau Timida, waits patiently by the door, just as the queen had asked of her loyal friend. However, Amala can feel Beau's growing impatience. She has work that needs to get done this evening, and Amala is stalling, dragging this time out with her daughter longer than she had promised.

The queen had frightened her daughter today, and she isn't sure how to approach the subject. There is no easy way. How does a parent tell a child they were at fault? How does a mother describe to her daughter how ugly this realm is and that she'll have to learn to be brave no matter what?

Davan and Amala have told Nefari she's Fate-blessed, but Nefari doesn't truly understand what that means. She doesn't understand that the kingdom is in danger because of her, a truth Amala will never reveal to her daughter. This sort of responsibility shouldn't fall on such a young girl's shoulders, royalty or not.

Amala thought she would have more time than this. She at least hoped Nefari would have grown into her power before such a threat could arise. Maybe she can. Maybe Salix's army won't be able to breach the creep.

She sighs as all these maybes, hopes, and dreams soar away. That's all these thoughts are – Hope. Hope has abandoned the realm.

So, instead of immediately jumping to a conversation Amala can barely stand to think about herself, she contently strokes Nefari's hair with slow, even pulls. Each strand sparkles in the torch's light.

"Do I *have* to go to bed, Momma?" Nefari whines for the third time. She knows something's wrong. Amala is never this content to remain quiet.

"Nefari . . ." Amala chastises. "I already gave you my answer. Do not ask me again."

In Nefari's lap are two dolls. Gen Riversdale had sewn and gifted them to the young princess for her last birthday. Well used and slightly faded, she combs her fingers through the dolls' yarn hair, mimicking her mother.

"Why can't I stay up a little later? Tomorrow's my birthday. I think I deserve it."

Amala grins at herself in the reflection of the vanity mirror. "You deserve it?" she repeats teasingly.

"Yes," Nefari says, meeting her gaze. She scrunches her little nose, knowing her mother finds her persistently stubborn personality endearing. Sometimes.

The queen reaches around and playfully pinches the tip of Nefari's nose. "In this realm, no one deserves anything. Nothing is fair. Nothing is just. It is never wise to fancy yourself deserving."

"Why?" Nefari asks.

Dipping down, Amala tucks a lock behind Nefari's ear and whispers, "Because, silly girl. All the good we receive in this life is a blessing, and all the bad is a lesson. But no one – you, me, not even your father – deserves what we have, for that is presuming we are better than others."

Nefari blinks at her mother, allowing the words to sink in. Amala had whispered because she knows quiet words are the loudest. Out of the corner of her eye, she can see her servant's small prideful smile. It is not uncommon for royals to see their servants as nothing but hired slaves in other reaches of the realm.

Nefari looks down at her lap. "And what about when we are afraid?"

"Are you afraid?" Nefari nods and sniffles. "What are you scared of?"'

"That the scary monster will come and get me, and I'll never get to see you again."

Setting the brush down on the vanity, Amala is quick to cup both hands against her daughter's warm cheeks and peer into her watery eyes. "Do you know what I want you to do when you feel alone and afraid, Nefari?"

She shakes her head.

Amala kisses her forehead. "I want you to be brave."

"I'm not brave. I'm not like you or daddy, momma. I'm not brave."

The queen tsks at her daughter and says, "I have something for you then."

Nefari tracks her mother's movements as she heads to the door where Beau waits, watching the exchange. First bowing, Beau passes Amala a tiny purple box. It's surface shines brightly in the reflection of the torches. Gingerly, Amala takes the box and thanks her by giving her elbow a light touch of appreciation.

Turning, she peeks adoringly at her daughter's questioning look while attempting to conceal the box behind her back.

Nefari stretches her spine, as if height will give her a better advantage to see what's being concealed. "What is it, Momma?" Dolls forgotten, Nefari allows them to drop to the floor as she scoots to the edge of her vanity bench.

"An early birthday present." Gathering up her skirts with one hand, she kneels on the stone floor and presents the tiny box to her daughter. The natural chill of the stone is uncomfortable, but the warmth filling Amala's heart chases it away.

Surprised, Nefari takes it from her mother's palm and opens the lid gently. A black diamond, smooth and inviting, winks at her, flashing like the shadow of fire, and she gasps. "It's beautiful!"

"Just like you," Amala says, her voice thick. She touches the black diamond. "It was mine, my mother's, and her mother's before that."

Nefari moves slowly as she pinches and removes it from the box. The ring is too large for Nefari to wear, so Amala had a chain fashioned for it. Amala takes the jewelry from her daughter, holds the chain just so, and slips it over Nefari's head.

"When you're afraid, I want you to press your lips to this ring and remember that you are as sturdy as the silver, as sharp as the stone, and as wise as all those who have worn it before you."

Wide-eyed, Nefari simply stares at the diamond.

"Nefari? You need to promise me."

"I will, Momma. I'll remember."

"That's my girl," Amala coos, using her thumb to wipe away a single tear that had escaped and slipped down her daughter's cheek.

A knock sounds at the door, and the hinges creak as it opens. Both royals turn to look as Amoon, Davan's niece and Nefari's friend, pokes her head through the opening. A wide grin spreads across her face when she meets Nefari's gaze. A touch of mischief glints inside them, but Amala has grown accustomed to the girl's need for adventure.

The queen turns back to her daughter and pats her knee. "Go. Help Amoon pick out one of your dresses for tomorrow." She kisses Nefari's nose. "That way, she can be a princess, too."

The girls giggle and disappear into the spacious adjoining closet, leaving Amala to speculate on her daughter's future.

Beau approaches. "Are you all right, my lady?"

"May my daughter truly be Fate-blessed," Amala whispers. "Because she's going to need every advantage she has."

"Indeed."

Chapter Eight

"I think this flower will suit my daughter well," Amala says to Beau. Today is Nefari's birthday, and it's the queen's job to have the final say on the decorations, agenda, entertainment, and so on and so forth. As nervous as she's been about this day, she's dreamed of it. An eighth birthday is an honor for any shadow person, and she wants it to go as smoothly as possible.

Beau bows and scuttles away with the flowers, directing a handful of other women. They begin the table arrangements with the flower of choice, accenting it with shades and colors that go well with the blue petals.

"Drape that a little lower," Amala shouts to those decorating the beams with ropes stringed of lanterns. Inside each lantern is the shining poisonous beetle, which will provide the nightly, starry effect the shadow people are known for. "Make sure it's secure, too. The last thing we need is for the ropes to slip from their hold and crash down on the heads of our guests."

"Yes, My Lady," they say in unison.

Amala places her hands on her hips, blows a stray lock of hair from her eyes, and turns to view the throne room. On the dais is the table where the royals and honored guests will sit. The table settings are already there, glistening with their polished shine. A servant preps the other tables with the same, but with smaller platters and plates. A small stage is being erected in the corner for the musicians, and the hammering of nails into wood is a steady pound to Amala's ears.

"My Queen," a familiar voice says. Amala turns, a grin on her face, and finds Gen already in a bow. Behind her are two shadow women, their arms full of garments.

Amala intervenes before they can attempt their bow. "Please, there is no need." She grasps Gen's hand. "Thank you for doing this. May I see what your brilliant mind has sewn?"

"Of course," Gen says nervously. Amala frowns at her shaky, unsure tone. Perhaps the stress of the day was too much on the older woman.

Gen waves to the women behind her, and they stagger forward. First, Gen pulls Amala's dress from the pile, holding the garment up for the queen's view.

"Oh," Amala gasps, running her fingers over the soft fabric of her deep blue dress. "This is lovely, Gen. You have outdone yourself."

"Thank you, My Lady."

There's a wavering to her voice Amala hasn't heard before. Instead of commenting on it, however, she presses on, her attention returning to the garments. "And Nefari's?"

Another dress is pulled from the stack in the other lady's arms. The dress is a lighter shade and stitched with a material that resembles tiny stars. "Oh," Amala gasps, grasping the dress by the shoulders and holding it out in front of her. She peeks over the neckline. "Oh Gen, she's going to love this."

Gen's bottom lip trembles with a weak smile. Frowning, Amala drapes the dress over the other garments and places a concerned hand on her shoulder. "Is everything alright?"

"Y-Y-Yes. Why do you ask?"

"You don't look like yourself, Gen. Is something bothering you?"

Gen swallows. "Everything is fine, My Lady."

Amala chews on the inside of her lip while she studies Gen's expression. The woman could never give a convincing lie, but Amala has no desire to push her either. Secrets don't always have to be shared.

"Very well," Amala says. She dismisses the women, and they bow as they back out of the throne room. Hoyt, having walked in a second before, pecks his wife on the cheek before continuing to Amala. He strides up to her, turns, and stands at her side. His head swivels as he observes the decorations.

"Is everything ready for our guests?" Amala asks quietly.

He nods once and then crosses his arms. "The royals arrived an hour ago. Those who are human have been seen to the guest quarters. The centaurs are preferring to stay in the Shadled while the crones have been housed in the guest homes behind us. Everything is as you wished it."

"Wonderful." Amala rubs her hands up and down her arms, suddenly chilly. "Have you –"

"I have. They've agreed to meet with you in an hour."

"Thank you, Hoyt."

He chuffs. "Don't thank me yet. I still don't think you should do this. It's dangerous."

Sighing, Amala pats him on the arm in a petulant manner. "A shadow queen can't be afraid of the dark."

Chapter Nine

Under the canopy of swollen, purple Shadled leaves and within their shadow, Amala scopes the quiet forest. The shadow feels like a warm blanket wrapped snugly around her, but it's much more than that. If someone were to look closely, they'd just make out the shine and shade of her hair and the sparkle of her black skin.

The forest doesn't feel so alive today. Perhaps it remembers yesterday. No creature peeps, scratches, or roars. No breeze stirs the branches. No guards march across the brittle packed dirt, and not a single hunter is in sight. It's just as Hoyt promised.

Amala blinks her relief. Slowly, she steps from its safety. Her muscles are cramped from standing in one position for so long, but with each stealthy stride, they loosen. The general location she wanted to meet the leader of the centaurs and the leader of the crones isn't far from here, but she knows better than to not remain alert.

According to the stories, crones are always on the hunt to feed their insatiable appetites. Amala has no desire to be anyone's next meal, wraith or crone alike.

74

A nervous energy flitters over her skin, but she shoves it aside. Now isn't the time to feel nervous or fearful. Now is the time to be brave. She wishes she had a black diamond ring to comfortingly press her lips against. The cool smoothness would be welcome compared to the sliver of doubt slithering under her skin. That had always been what calmed her as a child, and now she hopes it'll do the same for Nefari.

The cracked dirt reminds her of what her feet looked like. The cuts from the Sea of Gold had made Beau glare at her and the healer tsk chidingly. She winces to the echoing pain when a sharp chunk of dirt breaks away and presses into the arch.

Steadying herself against a trunk, she takes a moment to regain composure. Amala's thoughts continue to churn around the impending conversation, rolling arguments and scenarios around like the high winds of the Black Sand desert. There's an excellent chance both leaders will deny her request. If they do, she's out of options.

The forest is as bone dry and dark as it always is, but the Diabolus Beetles leisurely soar from one tree to the other, effectively lighting the path. Hundreds of them, maybe thousands, have gathered in the forest this morning. Their mere presence and lazy frolicking ease the frantic pace of her heart.

Soon, she finds her breathing becomes easier, her senses more dull. Despite the wraith attack, this forest has always been another home to her. Its familiarity works its way into her tense muscles and chases away any lingering fear she has.

A twig snaps.

The queen jumps and her hand glows with pulsing light. A large hoof presses into the beetle's illuminated path, followed by an equine's leg. The muddy brown fur fades into the leathery brown skin of a man's lower torso. Amala raises her gaze to the tattoos stretching across the torso. The etchings of the tattoos appear as though someone came along and stamped the skin with tree bark and leaves dipped in ink. She breathes a sigh of relief, knowing she has nothing to fear from the creature.

Bastian had once told her the design will change with their surroundings. Right now, as he steps into the beetles' light, they morph from the dark bark into a collage resembling the purple leaves of a young Shadled tree.

"Bastian," Amala greets breathlessly. She lowers her hand and the pulse of light absorbs back into her skin.

The centaurs' leader, Bastian Pike steps soundlessly into Amala's path. A twinkle of amusement glimmers in the set of his gaze and posture. His irises and lips are the same soothing shade of deep green summer grass.

"Are you alone?" She squints into the darkness.

"As you commanded," he answers. He bows respectfully, and long, dark red hair tied at the nape of his neck falls past his left shoulder. It shines like silk.

Strapped to his back are his bow and a leather quiver of large arrows, the color matching his hair. The bow is nearly her entire height, and when she was younger, it used to intimidate her. How can someone have the strength to pull such a taut string?

"Although," he continues, righting himself. "I didn't expect you to be startled."

"I didn't see you there." Amala glances around. "I was lost in my own thoughts. Besides, you shouldn't sneak up on people."

"As I recall, you were the one who asked me here, Queen Ashcroft." Bastian's wide upper arms bulge and ripple with muscle as he crosses his arms over his bare chest. A beetle lands on his thick leg, mistaking him for a tree, and he stomps his front hoof. It flies past his face, illuminating the scar slashed across his cheek.

Bastian has known Amala since she was an infant, and even more so when she was strong enough to hold a sword and wield her magic. Her father had commissioned him to train her in combat. She failed at it, according to Bastian's high standards.

As a child, Amala thought his only wish was to see her fail. She was certain he hated every fiber of her being and wasn't entirely sure why he was there in the first place. What had made him stay? What kept his patience? Her child-mind couldn't comprehend it.

However, when Amala grew into a teenager and a young adult, she had come to realize he was hard on her *because* he cared. All the bruises and cuts and barked orders were because he didn't want to do her the disservice of coddling. Coddling doesn't save anyone's life.

Amala had been more naturally adept at magic-wielding, lessons her father had taught, but Bastian refused to let that be her only means of protecting herself. Because of the need to make her more than what she was born to be, she has a special place in her heart and a deep respect toward the leader. It's the sort of respect only trust and honor can buy.

The centaur cocks his head to the side and blinks his slanted equestrian eyes at her. The action reveals the hilt of his sword sheathed across his other shoulder farthest from Amala. At the angle he stands, she hadn't seen it before. Why had he come so prepared?

"Why did you call us here?" Bastian asks, pulling her gaze from the worn hilt of his sword.

Amala frowns. "Us?"

"You have been slacking on your training, young one." Bastian expresses his disappointment with a contemptuous curl to his top lip and points up.

Slowly, the queen tilts her head back. Perched on a branch, Wrenchel Withervein stares down at them. A single beetle rests against the trunk as if warning them she's been there the entire time and refusing to let the woman linger in complete darkness.

Wrenchel's sharp pointed teeth, rotted and decayed, are bared in a feral grin. Straw-like grey hair sticks out in every direction, and her clothes are aged, soiled, ripped, and burned in the oddest places. The hag looks like she hasn't eaten in days, for her skin hangs off her bones like her rags hang off her body.

"You smell deliciously sweet," she says, each word slow, deep, and snake-like. When she emphasizes the word sweet, Amala's skin crawls. "Like the ripe melons grown in the fertile soils of Salix."

Amala backs up a step.

The crone scuttles across the tree's upper trunk like a spider, and Amala flexes her hand at her side. Magic pulses at her fingertips, dancing around each nail.

Wrenchel laughs in delight. "Are you frightened, child?" The crone, now near enough to the base of the trunk, drops down. She lands on her feet as if the frail and alarming twists of the joints in her back are just for show. The portion of her spine between her shoulder blades is hunched, and the wrinkles on her forehead ripple away from her eyebrows until they disappear into the hairline.

Her eyes are wild. Yellow and wild. Amala's instincts beg her to run.

"It has been a long time since I tasted fear in the air and an even longer time since I tasted it within the flesh. Ripe melons indeed."

Amala was beginning to think this was a mistake. She only needed Wrenchel for her seer abilities, but perhaps Amala could have found another way to discover a morsel of the future. Hoyt was right to steer her away from this meeting. She shouldn't have the crone thinking about her daughter in any way.

Nefari's skewered corpse turning over a blazing fire flashes in Amala's mind, and she has to shake her head to rid herself of the image.

Just one detail. Amala just needs one detail so she knows the direction to take for her daughter and her kingdom.

Wrenchel slinks closer, muscles tense for a lunge.

Just then, a dagger flies through the air. The crone gasps as it stabs through the drooped armpit of her tunic and straight into the trunk of the tree behind her. The crone tugs and hisses at the palm-sized blade, but it's embedded too deep.

"I'm not afraid of you," Amala says, steeling her nerves. "There are more important things to fear than the leader of the crones and her hunger for flesh."

"Release me, centaur!" Wrenchel growls.

Bastian lowers his hand from his aim. "Do not threaten the Shadow Queen, Wren. She may be young, but I was the one who trained her. She will not hesitate to kill you if it protects her daughter or her people. Believe me when I say I taught her exactly that."

"Fools," Wrenchel cackles. "Nobody can escape death."

"It isn't me who needs to escape death," Amala mutters, eyeing the crone as if she were a caught and unpredictable wild hog. A shadow crown appears on Amala's head, dancing and flaring, the wispy points acting like the hot tip of a flame.

The crone whips her gaze to Amala and considers the shadow crown. "Why did you call me here?"

"Because I need your help. Both of your help."

"Why would I help you?" the crone asks. She blinks quickly, once, twice, and after the third, a dawning expression smooths her wrinkles. A knowing sort of amusement twinkles in her yellow irises, and she relaxes against the trunk, laughing. "I see your desires, Shadow Queen. Foolish. Despite what the legendary centaur implies, you are foolish. Hopeful, young, and *foolish.*"

"You owe me a favor," Amala grumbles fiercely, hoping to regain control over the situation. This could spiral out of control far too easily. She steps toward Wrenchel with an accusatory jab of her finger. "Our laws had demanded that we kill your kind on sight if we caught you lurking without invitation. When your sister ate these beetles," she swivels her finger, gesturing to the Diabolus Beetles, "and dropped half-dead on this very forest, I was the one who nursed her back to health in secret. I was the one who made the antidote. I was the one who saved her from a certain and painful death. *You. Owe. Me.*" Amala's voice is gravelly with the ferocity of her emotions.

The crone glares, observing the sparkles along her skin that fluctuated with Amala's last three words. "There are many things I could give you, Shadow Queen. Your daughter's safety isn't one of them."

"I'd never ask you to harbor a common child," Amala spits. She knows they'd be flayed alive and eaten raw. "Harboring a royal child wouldn't even be entertained."

"Then what do you want from me?"

Amala straightens her shoulders. "A vision."

Bastian calls Amala's name in warning. "You shouldn't trust the crones. Especially this one. They're Despair born."

"Despair born or not, I need guidance only a seer can give." Amala half-turns to him. He keeps his expression blank, knowing he has no sway over her decisions.

"Very well," the crone says slyly. "But I want a favor in return."

"No." Amala whips her head back to Wrenchel. She cuts her hand through the air in emphasis. "You owe me. I don't owe you anything."

"Sight into the future would cost a great deal more than my sister's life." The crone leans forward and whispers quickly. "We do not cherish our own the way you weaklings do. I do not care that you nursed my sister back to health." She leans back into the tree. "If you mean to bargain, then let us bargain. It is not Raygelle you are striking a deal with."

Amala flexes her jaw and curls her fingers into fists. "What do you want in return?"

Wrenchel blinks innocently. "I want an escort through your castle. A tour, if you will."

The Shadow Queen hisses in outrage and frustration. No one, not a single Despair born, has been inside the Shadow Castle's halls. Sure, they're often invited to large celebrations in the shop's streets or the throne room, but they usually never show. Not once have they been inside the portions that house the royals. Not once have they stood inside the great library or the treasure room. It would be a breach of security. Who would feel safe with a cannibal absorbing every detail of their fortress?

"Amala," Bastian drawls, warning her to say no. It reminds her of Hoyt and his need to order her around. She bristles

82

at it. It's the sole factor that sways her weighing decision from an outright no.

"Done," Amala says, jutting her chin.

"Good. Then the bargain is struck. What future do you wish to hear? Yours perhaps? Your husband's?" A wicked grin exposes her rotting teeth. Amala scents the decay, and her top lip curls.

"You know full well that I want my daughter's. No games, crone. Only truths. Otherwise, I'll assume your seer's ability cannot stretch as far as you like to boast, and our bargain will dissolve."

Wrenchel tips her head back and laughs. Amala swears the Shadled trees tremble because the sound is anything but joyful. Then, she sags against the tree's trunk and smirks at the two of them.

Bastian shifts his weight for a better position to grab the hilt of his sword.

"Threats. They taste as fine as fear." She sucks in a breath, blinks, and continues. "Of course I can see her future, but you can't blame me for a little distraction. The realm may not know about your daughter's fate, or rather, what Fate bestowed upon your daughter, but the three crone factions certainly do. I am not the only one of my people who has seen her future."

Amala bristles. The three crone factions are divided by territory in the northern Frozen Fades, each having their own leader and then one leader who governs over them all: Wrenchel. She, and she alone, has the final say when it comes to the crones as a whole. Each faction of crone is more disturbing and feral than the last, and over the years, they've been nothing but vicious. The stories that spread like wildfire through Amala's kingdom frighten even the most seasoned warrior.

"Then tell me," Amala demands.

The crone closes her eyes. "She will shape the darkness – this Fate-blessed princess of rage and wrath – for she is the crown of endless night and the memory of woeful shadows. Echoes of clinking chain and metal. The sharp sting of leather. The bitter taste of tears will feed despair, but the hopeful shards of a broken kingdom will find the fated queen, and then . . ."

"And then what?" Amala shuffles closer, fingers trembling. "Then what, Crone?"

Wrenchel opens her eyes. The yellow shade animates her glee. "Death will yawn and swallow the realm."

Chapter Ten

The Shadow Council and the array of important visitors and guests decorate the dais. Some are seated while they smile and pick politely at their meal. Others raise boisterous laughter while leaning against the long table stretched out before them, mug of ale in hand. The Kings and Queens have all arrived from Urbana, Sutherland, and Loess, and Amala watches as Bastian makes a point to greet each in turn.

The legendary centaur, as the crone liked to call him, has refused to meet her gaze since she toured Wrenchel through the castle. Her husband's anger over it hasn't gone unnoticed, either. She can feel Davan's rage from where she sits, but she refuses to bring more attention to it than what's already obvious.

Does he expect her to do nothing about what they've learned? Amala would strike a deal with Despair if it'd do any good. She'd do anything to protect her daughter. She's just thankful the throne room's darker interior hides the scarlet of his cheeks. It helps conceal his tantrum.

Lifting her goblet, she sips daintily at the wine, thankful it isn't the awful ale. The ale came from the Kadoka

Mountains, a gift from the centaurs. Though, certainly not a gift suitable for an eight-year-old princess's birthday. It is, however, appropriate for the betrothal announcement, which was bellowed by Hoyt and Davan before all sat to eat.

Amala grins into her cup, remembering her daughter's blush and the prideful puff of Vale's chest.

The wild boar was carried in by King Breyton of Sutherland's servants. Sutherland is a beautiful land, she's told, tropical and just south of the equator. The boar is seasoned with spicy herbs, and every now and then she can see her kitchen servants trying to guess at their names, heads bent in a conspiratorial sort of way.

More fruits were brought in by the King of Urbana, sir-named Uba. His queen had presented it to Nefari personally, pinching the youth of her cheeks in doing so. Amala can still smell the lingering citrus aroma from where they lie in baskets that line the wall behind the thrones. No doubt they were picked by the slaves. At least they didn't bring their slaves today. Amala wouldn't have let them through the castle doors.

Amala's attention flicks to King Genji. He and his wife are quiet, observing the festivities with guarded expressions. They've always been the quiet type. They had brought Amala's favorite, rare fish, which only swims in the shallow waters right outside Loess's sandy shore. They're expensive, therefore she hadn't had a single bite of the plentiful fish since her own eighth birthday. The meat is so rich that the time had not dulled the memory of their flavor.

She makes a mental note to thank them again for such a generous contribution.

All of this food is spread out across tables, including their own delectable dishes. Each platter seemingly represents the surrounding kingdoms with their aromas and presentations.

As the center focus of the room, Amala, Nefari, Davan, and Hoyt, Gen, and Vale can see the dance taking place before them. Due to the announcement, the Riversdales were asked to be seated at their dais table, a high honor within any kingdom. Their other sons are dotted throughout the spacious throne room, mingling, greeting, or conversing with friends or in Iger's case, potential lovers. Beau's back is against the wall, and she giggles quietly while Iger whispers in her ear.

Lutes, trumpets, and fiddles fill the space with joyous music fitting for the dual celebration. Most have finished with their meals and are dancing merrily to the music. No matter which kingdom they came from, they mix together, swaying with one another in proper formation. Soon, the traditional shadow dance will take place, a special tribute to the guests and the celebration. It is Nefari and Amoon's favorite part.

A slow-moving figure, hobbling and limping with obvious age, catches the attention of the queen. Wrenchel and a few of her sisters move throughout the crowd beginning to form around the dancing partners. Their expressions are blank, but every now and then, they stop to have a hushed conversation. The mere fact that they're inside this castle sends Amala's skin crawling.

They were invited to come before I made the deal with their leader, Amala reminds herself, but somehow, now that Wrenchel has seen the halls and the rooms and every entrance, it feels . . . different.

She looks to Hoyt. He's watching them with a shrewd expression, clenching his mug of ale so tight she fears the brazened clay may shatter and crumble in his hands. His mistrust is evident, and certainly not unwarranted.

Their gazes catch and a silent command is given by a single nod of Amala. She hears the flare of her shadow crown as her heart skips a beat, fearing the worst. The crone could cause a lot of trouble here tonight. It's best to have her watched closely. The last thing she wants is to have missing children.

Hoyt blinks his confirmation. His high back chair scrapes against the stone of the dais as he pushes it back, stands, and strides to the watchful Onyx Guard sprinkled strategically throughout the room. A few depart, slipping into the shadows to silently obey.

After the prophecy was dropped on Amala, Wrenchel had wrenched free of the dagger as if it never truly held her in the first place. Now, Amala can't help but wonder what angle the crone was playing. What did she gain from the exchange?

With a nibble on the edge of a freshly baked roll, Amala exhales through her nose. The Onyx Guard will alert her if they cause any harm. She shouldn't worry about it when this entire ball is to celebrate and honor her daughter. Most people aren't worried about the crones – they're seeing them as nothing but guests. Amala should follow their lead and try to appear less grave, if for no other reason than her daughter's concern.

Bastian and the handful of centaurs he brought with him surround the crowd, continuing to mingle socially with the guests. The white cloth bandage around Bastian's hand is a beacon for the curious, however. Just a moment ago, Davan had asked about it, in which Amala hadn't responded. Her daughter is in hearing distance, and today is meant to be a happy day for a young girl. Memories are important, and she refuses to continue to taint it. An eight-year-old doesn't need to know why the leader of the centaurs gave a blood vow.

Amala examines Bastian's bandaged hand and the small circle of blood that had leached through. After the crone had left, vowing to meet the queen in an hour, Bastian asked why he was there – why she asked to speak with him privately.

"I owe you more favors than you'll ever owe me," Amala had begun. She ran a hand through her hair, pushing her fingers straight through the shadow crown as if it was nothing but a mere shadow. "But I'm going to ask it of you anyway." Amala turned to him and peered up into his eyes. "A wraith made it through the shadows and entered my kingdom yesterday."

"Sieba Arsonian has found you," he had said bluntly. There was no surprise changing his expression. Amala nodded, and he continued, "It was foolish of you to ask the crone here. Sieba is possessed by Despair, and the crones are loyal to Despair."

"I know."

"Then you surely know that the crones are the ones who cast the spell across Salix. Magic is broken there. Weakened."

"Yes, I know. I've heard the rumors, too. You're not the only one with spies."

"Then why would you ask a crone here?"

"Because I have nothing left to lose. Queen Sieba knows where the Shadow Kingdom is now, and she knows how to get in. It's only a matter of time before she comes for my daughter. Speaking with a crone who will tell her everything about this meeting will not matter in the end, Bastian. She has information I need. Information that I could use to come up with a plan to keep my daughter safe."

"Then why did you call me here?"

Amala eyed the hilt of his sword. "To ask you to get my daughter to safety when the time comes. Stay in the Shadow Kingdom with me. Move in for a bit. We have the extra room, and I need more guidance than I currently have. I beg you, help me, Bastian. If – when – the time comes, get her and as many shadow children as you can to safety."

He had agreed then had vowed with his blood, a rarity for a centaur. It had taken Amala by surprise and her worries had eased a fraction. The action includes spilling blood to the ground and verbally vowing. It is an unbreakable promise surrounded by fated magics, and when the beetles had felt this magic, they had risen, swarmed, and then fled the forest.

Now, Amala looks to her daughter and smiles as she and Vale snicker and poke one another. Amoon is across the table, having joined them from Davan's sister's table seconds ago. She stands, leans her hips against the table, and rests her chin in her hands as she watches the two with a radiant smile.

Amoon and Nefari look so much alike. Anytime they're near one another, they're often mistaken as each other. The shadow tiara is sometimes the only way to truly tell them apart.

Leaning, Amala whispers to her daughter. "Why don't you take Vale and Amoon to dance with the others?"

Nefari's nose scrunches, and her tiny shadow crown splutters her disgust. "No!" she cries, her cheeks reddening. Amoon giggles behind her hand.

First swirling the contents, Davan sips from his goblet of wine. "It's your birthday, Nefari. We'll be going out into the courtyard soon for the shadow dance, which means the ball is almost over. Go. Enjoy it while you can."

Hoyt approaches patting his belly. His wife looks up to him and gracefully stands. She folds his fingers into hers, and he lovingly kisses her knuckles. Waggling his eyebrows secretly to her, he turns to the children and says, "Come, you three. It's time to teach you a proper dance." He grabs Vale by the back of his tunic and Nefari by the hand. Amoon trails along, an extra skip in her step.

Alone, Amala's foot taps nervously under the table. The thickening silence between her and her husband could battle the humid climates of Sutherland.

"When are you going to trust me with your secrets, Amala?" Davan finally asks quietly. He's surveying the festivities, but his hand grasps hers within her lap. His thumb strokes across her hand, and it surprises Amala, momentarily breaking her proper composure.

She regards him, nothing more than a sidelong glance, and searches her husband's expression as she works to find the right answer. "I do trust you, but the less who know about Nefari's future and my plan to secure it, the better. Besides, you needn't worry. I have it under control."

In truth, she doesn't. After hearing the crone's foretelling then giving her a tour, the most she had planned for the future was to get Bastian to move in. But her husband didn't need to know that. The rest can be planned tomorrow or the next day or the next. She has time. Whatever the Queen of Salix has planned, she won't be able to accomplish it for a while. Crossing Widow's Bay isn't something that can be rushed, especially with an army.

"I am your husband," he mutters.

"You are a man who has doubted me from the beginning," she says evenly, calmly. "I love you, Davan. Never doubt that. But I will not sit back and be idle, content to let the future unfold the way Fate had warned. This is my duty. A duty that will fall on our daughter's shoulders if we can manage to keep her alive long enough to become the queen she's meant to be." Amala was beginning to develop an abundance of anger toward Fate and all that he had left her daughter.

Death will yawn and swallow the realm. What does that even mean? Amala prays it isn't literal.

"So you do not trust me," he says with obvious sadness.

"I do not trust the ears around us. I do not trust anyone except for those who have been loyal to me my entire life." She looks to Bastian now, and Davan doesn't miss it. She can feel his sadness in the slow way his thumb traces circles on the back of her hand.

Silence falls between them again, and a knot forms in the queen's throat.

Oh, how it hurts to not confide in the man she loves. But she can't. She can't because he's spent Nefari's entire life not trusting Amala and her warnings.

After the next song, Davan nods his head slowly and squeezes her hand once. "Okay."

"Okay?" she responds distractedly, watching as Gen takes Nefari and Vale from the throne room. It's time for them to change into white silks for the shadow dance. During the shadow dance, the two will join in the tangled web of swaying shadows. Thus is the tradition.

Amoon stays behind, content to dance merrily with Hoyt, who was never blessed with a daughter. It's a shame, but at least he has the girl to dote upon.

"Keep your secrets, but I ask one thing of you." Amala turns her head to face him. "Whatever safety measures you have planned for Nefari, I ask you to take them with her. If Queen Sieba comes for her, I want you to escape with Nefari. I don't care if it's fifty years from now. Forget the kingdom. Forget me. Flee with our daughter."

"I won't –"

Davan shushes her soothingly. "We don't know what Fate's magic will do to Nefari's natural magic. She will need her mother's guidance for that, whether she be an eight-year-old, or a sixty-year-old. She needs her mother. I won't leave her to her own path in fate. I would sleep much better at night knowing that if this day were to ever come and our kingdom should ever fall, my wife and my daughter will make it out alive."

Amala closes her eyes as her chest pangs with hurt. He cups the side of her face with his large, warm hand, and she leans into his palm. Nodding, she feels her stomach churn, and she bites her tongue to contain her possible lie. Bastian will be the one to get Nefari to safety. That's what he had vowed.

Despite the loud noises of great revelry and music, Amala hears the high-pitched keening from the horses in the stable. The stable isn't far from the castle, but even so, Amala has only heard a horse make that sound once: when it fell, body twisting like a beetle stuck on its back, down a cliff overlooking Widow's Bay. The horse never rose again.

The queen opens her eyes questioningly. Her gaze lands on Wrenchel whose yellow irises are pinned to her. Amala startles at the sudden closeness of the crone. A wicked thump pounds her heart in uneven rhythms, her instincts telling her something is wrong before her thoughts can register it.

Wrenchel is at the corner of the royal table, and her feral grin exposes the wretched decayed teeth. As soon as Amala frowns over it, the windows behind her shatter.

Davan abruptly stands, shielding his wife from the shower of glass. Through his arms, Amala can see the wraiths pour in through the glassless windows. Deafening screams erupt in the throne room, causing goosebumps to rise across the queen's skin. As the last of the glass hits the stone, Amala abruptly stands with Davan.

The crone is gone. Utterly gone, and the throne room has descended into chaos as people run for cover.

Fear pumps through her veins so quickly that her body feels numb. "Davan! We have to get to Nefari!"

Davan does not answer. Amala whips around to face him, knocking her throne clean over. "Dav —" she stops abruptly. Her heartbeat thumps in her ears. The king does not watch her. He does not watch the wraiths swarming above. Instead, his hand clutches the bloody sword protruding from his belly.

Slowly, he raises his gaze to hers. "Amala," his mouth forms. "Run."

His body bows as the sword is pulled from his spine.

"No!" Amala screams. The King drops to the dais and Amala follows, slamming to the stone on her knees. Blood pools, rivering to Amala's knees, soaking into her silk dress. "No!" she screams again.

Placing her hands on his wound, she presses down. "I need a healer!" Amala screams, but it's absorbed by the crowd's terror.

Davan's breathing is ragged. Tears of pain and sorrow gather in his pinched eyes and stream down his paling cheeks. He blinks sluggishly and twitches his lips into a smile. "I-love-you," he says, reaching a hand to touch her cheek. His touch is weak, barely perceptible. Blood transfers from his fingers to her skin. "I – I –"

With a final breath, the king's body slackens. His hand falls to the stones with a thump.

"No!" Amala screams. Enraged, full of woe, she looks to who holds the sword. Surprise crosses her face, and she slowly leans away from her husband's corpse.

"Gen?" The queen's voice cracks. "Wh-Wh-What are you doing?"

"I didn't want to," Hoyt's wife says. Her voice is barely audible above the screams. "I didn't want to!" The tip of the sword leans heavily toward her feet. Amala knows the woman can wield one. As Hoyt's wife, he had made sure she could protect herself, but perhaps the weight of what she had done is causing it to feel heavier than usual. Where she snatched the sword from, though, Amala will never know.

"What have you done!"

"They have – They have –" Tears stream down Hoyt's wife's cheeks. "They said they'll keep my family alive. The crones. They promised. I'm sorry. I'm sorry."

Understanding crosses Amala's face. *The crones.* They turned the Captain of the Onyx Guard's wife against the kingdom. They had played on a mother's heart. As Hoyt's wife, she would know of the true goings-on in this castle. Did she tell the crones and wraiths when to strike? Who to strike first? Or did they tell her?

This morning, when she had brought the garments . . . she had been acting odd.

The crones . . . this is why Wrenchel wanted the tour.

A fool. *I'm a damn fool,* Amala thinks. No doubt every entrance is sealed. Perhaps even more wraiths or crones are waiting there to pick off those who flee. And the royal visitors . . . This ball was a trap the crones didn't have to lay.

"The Queen of Salix never needed to cross Widow's Bay, did she?" Amala growls, fighting the tremble that's seeping into her bones.

With difficulty, Gen swallows and raises the sword once more, a sob wracking her body. "I don't want to do this, My Queen. But I have to. I have to. My sons must survive what you have done."

What I have done? Amala blinks again.

"The prophecy. Death will yawn and swallow the realm. The crone told me. Half the kingdom knows. I can't. I won't. My sons must survive!"

Amala holds up a hand and falls on her rump. She has no weapon. No means of protecting herself. Her magic – she could use her hot light, but – Gen. She had trusted Gen.

She had always viewed Gen as a sort of mother when her own had died. Amala feels her heart breaking, cracking. Shattering.

"Let me help you! It's not too late. Let me help you!"

The woman shakes her head. "You can't. You've done enough!"

"Gen, wait. Wait!" the sword swings and Amala circles her arms protectively around her head. When two heartbeats pass without the sword slicing into her skin, she peeks past her arms, and the first thing she sees is Gen's body crumpled next to Davan's. Her head lies two feet away, rolled to its side between Hoyt's feet. Blood drips from the Captain's sword.

Hoyt had killed his wife.

Amoon sobs next to Hoyt's thigh, clutching the back of his tunic, and Amala gathers herself to her feet. She doesn't know what to say to him. Should she thank him? Grieve for him? Hug him?

She can do none of those things, because around her, blood sprays and cries of pain and death bounce off the walls as if they, too, are trying to escape the massacre ensuing. Swords clank against swords. Crones scuttle up the walls like spiders, choking the shadows as they stand within them, effectively cutting off any shadow person who tries to flee.

Amala can only hope some escaped.

"Run, Amoon!" Amala says to her. "Run and hide!"

Chapter Eleven

The hooves of the centaur's clap against the throne room's stone floor as they race to the dais. Amala watches as one, two, then three of them scoop up children, set them on their backs, and gallop past Amala.

"Orders, my lady!" Hoyt says. Amala can't fathom it, but he seems to have shoved aside his sorrow whereas Amala's has nearly blinded her senseless.

The wraiths dip from above, swarming after the centaurs. Instinctively, as her father had taught her, Amala raises her hands. Her magic blasts from her palms and pushes the wraiths back toward the high ceiling, hurdling them straight into beams. It's as though they're made of nothing but smoke and magic because the beams cut straight through them.

The centaur's hooves then crunch against the shards of glass. They leap from windows and onto the courtyard to the safety of the creep.

"Do you truly need orders?" Amala barks at him. "Gather the Onyx Guard! Get as many as you can to safety! Find places for the royal guests to hide! Arm as many as you can!"

It breaks Amala's heart to think about it, but saving the other royals above her own people is prudent. If the other royals were to die tonight . . . well, Amala's kingdom isn't the only one that would be conquered. Death may swallow the realm before Nefari's fate can get to it.

Swallowing thickly, she glances at her husband's corpse. His blood has trailed to her feet and she can feel it slide between her toes. She bends and grabs Gen's sword still slick with red.

"What about your daughter?" he yells, preparing himself to leave.

"I'll find her!" Amala wipes at her wet cheeks as she wildly searches for her daughter in the chaos of the running crowd.

Just then, an army dressed from head to toe in black pushes through the throne room doors. "Impossible," Amala whispers. She can feel the blood drain from her face.

"She's here," Hoyt adds gravely. "Queen Sieba's army is here."

It's not possible. It's not – How?

Hoyt dashes into the crowd, dodging and weaving between the clashing of swords, the scuttle of flesh-feasting crones, and the attack of wraiths. Bodies drop, seemingly sucked down to the floor as they wheeze their last breaths while clutching at blood-stained wounds. Wraiths swoop in like vultures to pick apart the living, and a single touch from their dark fog-churning hands makes their victims scream with pain.

Amala turns her attention away from the Captain's back. "Nefari!" she shouts above the screams. "Nefari!" Gen had been with her daughter and Vale, her own son. Did she hide them? Did she turn Nefari over to the crones? How far did the woman go to betray her own people?

"Amala!" The queen whirls to the call of her name. Bastian fights his way through the crowd. Amala doesn't miss it when his hoof squishes into the body of Queen Genji.

Bastian's overly large sword sings as it clashes with the approaching Salix army. Every second that ticks by, they get closer and closer to the thrones. Everyone, every person in this room, is being cut down as though they're fish in a barrel.

"Behind you!" Bastian shouts to her.

With a bereaved scream, Amala whirls, a dance so reminiscent of the dance of shadows her daughter will never get to see. The sword gleams, pulses with her power, and she slices it into the gut of a nearby warrior dressed in all black. Blood sprays, splats, hot, against her face, and the man falls backward. He trips over her husband's corpse, and his mask slips from his face.

Amala halts her next swing to decapitate the man. Halts, and blinks. The white hair . . .

Before her is her own kind. Before her, clutching his gut, blood pumping between his fingers, is a shadow man. His eyes are vacant, possessed, fixed on absolutely nothing.

They – they – they built their army from within. The Queen of Salix's wraiths possessed her own people. She didn't need to send an army. All she needed was the wraiths to

101

get inside . . . And while they danced and celebrated, her own people were being prepped to destroy the kingdom.

The sounds around Amala fade as she comes to a realization. She did this. Gen was right. She truly is to blame. Stuck solely on her daughter's future, she didn't see the whole picture.

She glances around, surveys her people who cry out, beg, or try to uselessly defend themselves against wraiths. Families are torn apart. Wives sob over their husbands' bodies only to get a sword in their backs. She watches one woman in particular as she screams at the touch of a wraith. Amala takes a step back. The woman's cries fade and she, too, becomes fixed on absolutely nothing. Her expression of pain morphs into a serene blank canvas. *Utterly possessed.*

Amala yells as pain laces through her calf. Her knee bends and hits the stone with cracking force. Her sword clatters to the ground and skids a few feet away.

Enraged, the queen looks behind her. The warrior who had tripped over her husband's corpse is standing once more, bleeding wound forgotten. Her eyes widen as his sword descends. It's met with another, ear-splitting metal against metal. Bastian's face is covered in the enemy's blood, and he uses his considerable force to shove the possessed shadow man back several feet.

Behind Bastian, Iger Riversdale turns, tears streaming down his face as he, too, realizes he's fighting his own people. He blinks at his mother's body once, follows the trail of blood twisting between the shards of glass, and it's enough. The slight tint of rose in his cheeks drains to the color of fresh downy snow. He falls to his knees beside her limp hand, and a crone seizes that moment to drop from the ceiling. She lands on Iger's back, rears her head back, and plunges her teeth into his neck. The crone was too quick, and it's too late by the time Bastian takes her head. Iger chokes on his own blood as he sucks his last few breaths then drops next to his mother's headless body, gaze fixed unseeing toward the ceiling.

Shakily, Amala gets to her feet and picks up her sword. She sucks in a quick breath when she accidentally puts weight on her injured leg. "Has any of your people gotten Nefari out?"

"No," Bastian says. His voice is robotic. Hopeless.

"Then why are you still here?" Amala barks at him. "Find my daughter!"

"I haven't been able to locate her in the crowd, dead or alive," he says. He grips her upper arm. "Where is she?"

"She's not here," Amala begins with a shake of her head. "Gen had escorted them out to change for the shadow dance. I have not seen them since." She wipes her face to rid the sweat from oozing into her eyes.

"Gen wouldn't have harmed them," someone says. Amala turns toward the voice. Hoyt, clutching a wound above his hip, breathes heavily. The remaining Onyx Guard are at his back, streaked with blood and white with fear.

"All the royals are dead, My Queen," an Onyx Guard says.

"She would have hidden them," Hoyt presses on. "Gen — She wouldn't harm a child. I know it."

103

"We have to find them," Amala says, believing him and the depth of the emotion seeping through his words.

"Not we," Bastian adds.

"Just you?" Hoyt exclaims. "Absolutely not!"

Amala fully turns to Bastian, and her expression smooths with understanding. With one final squeeze to her upper arm, he nods his farewell.

"No!" Hoyt presses. "Amala, you must go with him!"

But Amala shakes her head, a small, slow gesture. Both Bastian and she know that she can't. Not everyone in this room will survive, but she might be able to save a few. With her magic, she can save more than the Onyx Guard could. "I have a job to do, Hoyt. And so do you."

These words startle the captain, and within two blinks, he bows his head. Not for a gesture of respect. No. The way his head dangles between his shoulders, he knows she only tells the truth. And he knows both of their heartbeats are numbered.

"Goodbye, my friend," Bastian says.

"Save my daughter," Amala chokes. She grasps his hand, feeling the calluses, which feel rougher than they ever have before. "Hide her. Keep your vow to me."

Amala can hear Hoyt bellow to the guards, beseeching them to run. Someone must survive. Anyone. The shadow people cannot end here.

With a flex of his jaw, Bastian rears, turns, and thunders down the steps of the dais.

Hoyt pulls her attention back to the matter at hand. "The wraiths, my lady," he says, eyes to the black ghost-like creatures swooping, diving, and picking off the remaining sane. The sounds the wraith produce are like nothing on this realm. "They must be destroyed, or this entire kingdom will fall. No one will be able to escape."

The queen blinks as it hits her. If they're still alive, the children will be hunted through the forest until they're all dead. That is, if any centaurs carrying the children made it through the creep.

"Can you do it?" his voice is quiet, fading in and out as if it's a struggle just to remain upright.

Swallowing thickly, Amala studies the doors of the throne room, broken and barely remaining tethered to the wall. Somehow, Bastian had already disappeared through them. Somewhere in this castle, her daughter hides. Her heart. The love of her life. Amala's sole purpose of living.

Her heart longs to follow Bastian, tugs in that direction in hopes she'd keep the false promise to her husband and survive with her daughter. That was minutes ago. So much has changed in the span of a few minutes.

Amala squares her shoulders. She can't. She is the Queen of Shadows, and she has an obligation to her people.

Or what's left of them.

"Yes," she finally answers. It'll take a considerable amount of power. It'll take all of her. It'll kill her. To destroy this many wraiths and unleash all of her magic . . . It will kill her.

But at least, it'll be a far less painful death than she'd have if she were left to the wraiths or crones.

Chapter Twelve

Bastian bursts through Nefari's bedroom doors. The wood splinters, cracks, and groans as they fall from their hinges and to the floor. A servant ducks beside Nefari's vanity, her hands over her head. Beau, if he recalls correctly. She screams at the abrupt intrusion. The sound grates on every last nerve of Bastian's.

"Run!" Bastian tells her. She peeks at him from under her arms. He slashes his own through the air, pointing the tip toward the hall. "Run to the creep! Leave!"

Tears streaming down her face, she darts past Bastian and out of the castle's safety. Bastian knows she most likely won't make it outside of the castle. If the woman had half a mind left, she'd use the shadows in the hall to escape.

"Nefari!" the centaur screams. "Vale!"

A servant – a cook if Bastian had to guess – had reassured him that Gen had brought the children here. He hears a sound inside the child's closet, and just as he's beginning to stride toward it, an entirely different sound stops him.

He jolts as little arms wrap around his leg. The young girl sobs into his fur, and the centaur sighs in relief. "Nefari?"

The little girl looks up and Bastian blinks then frowns. The resemblance is striking, but this girl is not Nefari. "Amoon."

"You shouldn't be -" He had seen them dancing together earlier. Amala had told him how the girl idolizes the princess. Why would she run here? How did she get past the wraiths? *How did she get past the crones* is the better question.

"I want my mommy!" the little girl cries. Her elegant dress is ripped and stained with splatters of red.

Bastian bends to the little girl, sweeping her hair back from her face sticky with wet tears. "She will be along shortly," he lies. "But you need to run. Can you do that for me, little one? Can you run?"

Amoon shakes her head. Bastian had forgotten the smaller children cannot shadow jump. How is he going to get this little girl out of here when his sole purpose is to find the princess?

"Will you save me?" the little girl asks, her bottom lip protruding. "Will you help me find my mommy?"

He hears a noise again from within the closet, his heart leaping with joy. "I can try." Perhaps he can make this work. If the girl stays close, he can get Nefari and make a dash for the creep. He's carried full men before. Two little girls should be easy.

When he stands full upright, a stench stuffs itself up his nose. Centaurs have excellent senses, far better than they let on. He smells the crone before he sees her, smells the rotting stench like a carcass cooking in the dry heat.

"Bastian?" Amoon whispers, confused about the fear she's sensing from him. The tattoos on his stomach – rough etchings of stone – darken to a near shade of black as if to blend him with the shadows.

The centaur leader says nothing to the queen's niece. Instead, he tightens his grip on his blade. The calluses along his palm pinch painfully with the tight hold, and the edge glints in the flickering torch lights that line Nefari's spacious room.

The cackle comes first. Then, the crone slithers from the dark hall and glides one step into the bedroom. Her withered body is hunched, but her deeply wrinkled face is bright, and not in a good way. The wrongness of her emotions creep over Bastian, and he fights back a shiver when the crone licks her lips at the sight of the frightened little girl.

"Step aside, crone." It is not Wrenchel as Bastian had first believed but, instead, a younger version of her. A sister perhaps? Amala had said Wrenchel had a sister.

"We do not take orders from our enemy," the crone says. Bastian's stomach turns at the word 'we.' Two more crones skitter through the doorway, pulling away from the shadows like darkness itself. They crawl along the bedroom walls, all four limbs bent awkwardly, wrongly.

"We take orders from our Divine," one of the wall crone's says. "Don't we, Raygelle."

"Despicable," Bastian spits. He tucks the young girl between his two front legs and prays that those in the closet remain silent. "The Shadow Queen called you here out of the kindness of her heart, and instead, you sold her secrets to her enemy."

The three collectively laugh. The sound seemingly slips up the walls, caressing the ancient stone of the castle. The child shudders from it.

"She called us here for her own selfish reasons, centaur. We are hungry women and are loyal to whoever provides. Despair feeds us. Despair provides. Your queen does not."

Amala has never been Bastian's queen, but he doesn't correct Raygelle. "Despair only provides when it's for his own gain. Nothing good will come of the destruction of the Shadow People. You have made a grave error this evening."

Not only will the queen die, but the neighboring royals have died. Bastian does not know what this means for the future of the realm, but it cannot be good. He had long suspected the Queen of Salix would try to snatch the western lands for herself, possessed by Despair or not.

"Oh, that is where you are very wrong," Raygelle hisses. She coils her body in tight like a snake before it attacks. "Fate is gone, and the only semblance left of him is inside that little girl." She points to Amoon.

Bastian blinks and then peers down at the child. *They think she's Nefari.* The centaur blanches as a plan reluctantly forms in his head. A plan that might break the blood vow. When a blood vow is broken, it turns the blood vow's scar

110

black, forever marking that individual as untrustworthy. As a traitor. As someone whose word means nothing.

He will be marked. By proceeding with his plan, he will be marked as a man without honor.

Steeling himself to hide his internal pain, he looks back to the crones. There is no choice. It's the only plan he has.

"The kings and queens of Sutherland, Loess, and Urbana are dead. The Shadow King is dead. The Shadow Queen *will* die. And with her child dead, Despair can rule the Divine Realm," Raygelle continues. "Despair will push to the reaches of the realm. And once that's completed, well. . ." She trails off, her words turning into a chilling chuckle.

Bastian backs up a step as Raygelle shuffles forward, widening the gaps between her and the two crawling along the walls. "And what of the other two Divine?" the centaur pushes. "Hope and Choice will never allow Despair to rule so completely."

Raygelle tips her head to the side. Her wiry hair resembles straw and doesn't move an inch with the movement. "Despair already has one of them, centaur. It is only a matter of time before Despair finds the other."

"Fools," Bastian barks. He swipes a hand through the air, frightening a squeak from Amoon. "All of you."

"Hungry fools," a crone on the wall chortles. "Young blood has always been our preferred diet. Shadow children are even better. Softer. Easier to chew. We will take pleasure in this. After we prove her death, we will come for you and your people next."

"Unless," the other wall crone drawls, grinning down at him.

"Unless?" Bastian asks patiently, itching to abandon his sword for his bow and arrows. All three of them would be dead by now if he had his bow and arrows.

"Unless you give us the child," Raygelle says. She licks her lips. "Give us the princess, and we will leave your people alone."

Just then, a clatter rattles within the closet. It's so quiet, he doubts a normal human would have heard it. Bastian's heart skips a beat as the crones look to it. Swallowing his heavy guilt, Bastian plucks the child from his leg, knowing she will provide the necessary distraction.

Divine help me, he prays.

"Deal," Bastian says. His heart shatters, and he can feel the strain of his blood vow as it begins to snap. He had promised to get as many children as he could to safety, and now he's breaking that promise by handing an innocent child over to the flesh-eating crones. Amoon won't survive this. They'll be giving a half-eaten body to the Queen of Salix with nothing but her face left intact for proof of death.

"Deal?" the crone says, almost disbelievingly. She hadn't thought he'd agree to the terms.

"Yes. Deal." He'll pay for this in more than just a dishonorable mark. He just knows it. Someday, he will pay for this sin.

Alarmed, Amoon gawks at the centaur, but he refuses to meet her gaze – the gaze that looks so much like Nefari's. Instead, he pulls her away from his legs, detaches her fingers from his fur, and shoves her toward the crones.

They pounce on the girl, and she screams so loud Bastian's ears pop. The tear of flesh sounds like the ripping of cloth and the scent of iron fills the room.

Chomping down his jaw, Bastian ignores it – or tries to, as he shoves the sounds echoing throughout his surroundings down deep, deep, deep until all he feels is nothing but numbness and the echoes of regret.

With the crones distracted, he gallops to the closet and wrenches open the door. There, curled under the skirt of her dress, is Nefari in her shadow form. Her shoulders quake as she silently sobs. Vale sits next to her, his arms protectively encircling her. He too is in his shadow form, his face set in a yawning expression of horror. Vale is old enough to understand what Bastian had just done.

"Hurry," Bastian says, urging the two children by holding out his unbandaged hand. The blood vow snaps like a twig and he grunts at the pain lacing his palm's wound.

"Hurry!" he urges again, then sheaths his sword.

Vale helps the princess to her feet then gives the girl a boost onto Bastian's back. They're both still dressed in their white silks meant for the shadow dance that they'll never get to partake in. It makes the centaur wonder what Vale's mother had told the children to convince them to hide instead of returning with her.

With more strength than Bastian would have thought from a young boy, Vale leaps onto the centaur's back and nestles tightly against Nefari's back.

Bastian peeks out of the closet. The little girl's screams have stopped, replaced by the sounds of breaking bones and screeching, bickering hags. They're bent over the body, gorging on the hot meat and slurping the blood. His stomach roils.

The crones still distracted, Bastian exits the closet as quietly as he can, picks up the vanity stool, and suffers a deep breath. "Prepare yourselves," he whispers, knowing the two children will hear him. They're sobbing at the sight of their friend's ravaged body and brutal death.

Upon his exhale, he hurtles the stool at the large window. The glass shatters, and the crones whip toward them, but Bastian's already galloping to his new exit.

"Hold on!" he shouts.

The centaur leaps, and as he does, several things happen at once. Bastian hears the whistle of arrows, a thud as it finds a target, and a man's shout. Inhuman shrieks. Shrieks that sound like pain instead of surprise. And Vale, in an effort to ward off the sound by covering his ears, falls from the centaur's back and onto the floor of Nefari's bedroom.

Nefari turns and cries his name, but they're already midway out the window.

Bastian lands on a cobbled path just outside of the castle. He pauses, just for a moment, and observes the dead bodies decorating his surroundings. White protruding bones. Red puddles. *Dead shadow people.* To his right is a centaur who had fallen on hip-height stone fence. Half of his side is eaten, and his intestines string down the fence.

"We have to go back!" Nefari yells, thumping Bastian on the shoulders. It stirs him from the horrors around him, from the scent of death tainting the air. "Vale fell! We have to go back!"

Bastian looks back to the second-story window, his hooves sliding against the cobbled stones. He can hear shouts of men among the dying shrieks of the crones.

"We can't." The centaur squares his jaw, hoping whoever is fending off the crones will be able to get the young boy to safety.

"We have to!" Nefari cries. Bastian doesn't listen. He doesn't say a word either. Nothing he can say to this child will ease what has happened today. Nothing he does will erase this from her memory, nor his, either.

Without a second thought, he turns and gallops toward the creep. Their fight is nowhere near over. Getting out of the Shadow Kingdom undetected is only a speck of hope, and Hope doesn't appear to answer prayers anymore. Perhaps Hope is the one who Despair had captured.

Chapter Thirteen

Hoyt watches as the extraordinary magic builds and builds inside the Shadow Queen. Every star fleck across her skin becomes blinding, too painful to stare directly at.

In the throne room, old shadows are banished, exposing the waiting crones, and new ones are formed. Shadow People dash to the new shadows, disappear inside them, and escape successfully to safety. For the first time during this siege, Hoyt allows himself to feel a sliver of optimism.

"It's working," he whispers to no one in particular.

Beau had told an Onyx Guard that Vale and Nefari were in the princess's chambers, and Hoyt had ordered the guard to help Bastian get them to safety. He can only hope the guard will succeed, for there is no way he will be following his princess or his son today. Instead, he will follow his wife to the afterlife where he will seek justice for her betrayal.

The captain slides closer to Amala, sword raised. He's prepared to defend her and her light so more may flee. His eyes drift to the broken chairs where his youngest son sat this evening. *Survive*, he mentally urges the memory of

Vale. *Survive. Protect the princess. Help her save the shadow people.*

Hoyt knows that those who escape this evening will not be safe. Not truly, nor completely. They'll have to hide. They'll have to run. They'll be hunted.

"Now, My Queen," Hoyt urges as the hair on his arms singes away. "Your light – I can't. It's burning – You must release it!"

Through the pockets of what's left of Amala's mind, she hears him. The magic inside her is excruciating, charring her organs. Smoke escapes from her nostrils, trickling along her skin. The pain consumes coherent thoughts. It burns at her rapidly beating heart. It's a living thing all on its own, and there's no stopping it now.

Memories flash through her mind. Images of her people in the midst of joy. Her daughter taking her first step. The day she married her husband under the blessing of Fate.

Amala looks to the wraiths. Blearily, she watches them possess her people, chase her people, taunt her people. They have yet to care about her bright light or understand that soon, it'll be their death. They care about nothing aside from their orders to destroy and possess.

She swallows once, tears springing to the pockets of her eyes, and says one final mental goodbye to the daughter she'll never get to see grow into the fine woman she knows she'll become. She then says a prayer to Hope and Choice, wherever they are, beseeching them to avenge all who died today.

"My Queen!" Hoyt shouts. A wraith dives toward them.

Screaming at the top of her lungs, Amala thrusts out her arms, and the brightness explodes from her body.

That's the funny thing about shadows, is Amala's last thought before the magic destroys her. *They cannot exist without light.*

Chapter Fourteen

Bastian's hooves pound against the cracked and dry Shadled Forest floor. It's a steady beat that mimics the slamming of his heart against the inside of his ribs. Nefari sobs against his spine, her arms wrapped tightly around his middle. The sheath for his sword is pressed into her cheek while the actual sword is once again clutched in his hand.

Ears strained for approaching wraiths or crones, the centaur dashes between the trunks. He's not fool enough to believe he's not being followed.

Occasionally, he yells for the young girl to duck when passing under a low branch, and she obeys immediately at the sternness of his tone. For an eight-year-old, she has a good grasp of the situation at hand. Her life is in danger, and it's his duty to get her to safety. On some level, through the shock, she knows this. Trusts him. Knows he's taking her away from everything she knows.

Nefari hasn't asked about her mother or father. She hasn't asked about her people. Seeing her cousin being eaten by the crones is enough to know the answer to any question she might have.

He heads toward the meeting point at the base of the Kadoka Mountains. It was discussed before the ball that if things were to ever unfold, this is where he and his people would meet. He would have never dreamed only hours after the conversation that the plan would be in motion.

The crones will never cross the blood-thirsty blades of the Sea of Gold, and if they tried, they'd bleed to death before they reached the base of the mountains.

"We're almost there," the centaur says to his young charge. His words come in huffs and puffs.

The ground rocks as though a quake were occurring below his hooves. Nefari screams, clutching to Bastian tighter. Her nails dig into the bare skin along his stomach. He doesn't feel the pain though. Instead, a nauseating wave of grief sweeps through him. A lump forms in his throat, and tears grease his vision. It's been a long time since the centaur has cried. He knows what this means. He knows that the ground shook because of a great release of magic. A terrible deal of magic. Magic which destroys the wielder in the process.

Bastian skids to a halt at the edge of the forest and peers back the direction from which they came. There are no beetles to light the path, but still, he can see one crone running along the branches on all fours, hopping from tree to tree. She's not deterred by the trembling ground or the scent of magic and death the seeps through the forest's shadows.

He blinks, keeping his eyes closed for just a second to mourn his friend. The tears spill down his cheeks, hot against already heated and flushed skin. They leave sparkling trails and glisten with a spiritual farewell to a fallen queen and kingdom.

"Bastian!" someone calls from across the Sea of Gold. "Hurry!"

Bastian opens his eyes, and with a sorrowful heart, he leaps onto the gold razor-sharp grass. He dashes for the snow-capped mountains with his charge rocking expertly to the motion of his gallop.

"She's getting closer!" Nefari warns. Her innocently terrified tone makes his blood chill.

"Help!" she screams to anyone who will listen as the crone leaps for Bastian. A centaur's arrow whizzes past Bastian's head, and Nefari's scream is cut short when the crone abruptly drops to the bladed grass. A kill shot.

With a flex of his jaw, Bastian vows to thank whoever made the lucky shot, for if the crone were to live, then Nefari's cousin's death would be all for naught. News would get back to Salix that Nefari is still alive, and Amala's sacrifice would be in vain.

A minute later, Bastian and the princess are with the other centaurs and their shadow charges. Bastian works to control his breathing, to push his fear and grief down to the darkest places of his tainted soul. His centaur companions eye him warily, gravely, waiting for his orders.

The children's faces reflect evidence of their shock, even those wearing their shadow forms in a futile effort to protect themselves from what had just transpired. Their kingdom is gone. Their parents are dead. As far as the centaurs know, they're the only living shadow folk to have survived.

The cold emitting from the snowy mountains and icy trail slides down the slope, and the surviving children shiver on the backs of the centaurs.

"Are they –" Nefari begins, turning her head, observing the forest that was once her playground. Bastian twists slightly to peer at her sidelong. Her posture is tense, and the night sky's stars twinkle just like her shadow form. She looks like a diamond. Like the black diamond ring draped around her neck, resting softly on a chain against the silk of her white dress.

In this very moment, the eight-year-old looks far older than she should have to be. Bastian's heart of steel cracks once more, witnessing her youth seemingly stolen from her.

Bastian's stomach twists. He had hoped they'd get back to his village before he had to start answering questions. The trees whose shadows hold all her memories will plague her dreams now. It'll morph every memory she has and turn it into a nightmare until what was once happiness is twisted with rage or sorrow. How is he going to explain this to her? How gently does he need to explain it?

"Are my parents dead?" she finally manages to ask. Her voice is empty and hollow.

Bastian's jaw ticks and he grips the hilt of his sword tighter. He decides to answer with the brutal truth. "Yes, child. Your parents are dead."

"And Vale?" Nefari asks. She swivels on his back to glance at each face of the shadow children. Vale isn't among them.

"I do not know."

"We have to go back," Nefari says urgently. "We have to go get him." She crawls off Bastian's back and starts to walk toward the Sea of Gold.

Bastian grabs her arm before she can cut her bare feet. "There is nothing to go back to, child. If Vale managed to – It's too dangerous – You won't make it across the grass before it kills you." He doesn't know how to convince her. He doesn't know how to break it down for a child to understand. Any way she were to look at it, she can't go back. She won't survive it.

She yanks her arm out of his grasp and angrily wipes at what remains of her tears. "Vale has to be alive!"

"Look around you," Bastian whispers patiently. He lowers his torso so he can peer more evenly in her eyes. "This is who is left of your people. This is who you need to look to. This is who you will lead." He reaches and tucks a stray white lock behind her ear. The lock is stained red with blood that isn't her own. Amoon's? Did her blood spray in the crone's frenzy?

Nefari doesn't notice the red, so Bastian doesn't point it out, nor let his gaze linger on it too long. "You are their queen now. Tuck your tears away, child. There will be plenty of time for that later."

"I hate you!" she yells abruptly. The ferocity behind it makes the other centaurs uncomfortable, and they shift their stances. "You should have saved my mother. You should have saved Vale. You sacrificed Amoon!"

Bastian blinks, sneaking a glance at his people. Confusion crosses their features. No doubt he'll be questioned about it later.

"I hate you," she adds quietly, and somehow, it has more meaning than if she were to shout it.

Bastian can't change the past, nor can he explain to her that there is no time to find a better way. No one had expected any of this. Not tonight. Not on her eighth birthday. The kingdom had assumed the Queen of Salix would need more time to get her army across Widow's Bay. She has no allies on this side of the realm. Her only choice was to ship the army or brave a march across the Frozen Fades. No one, not even Bastian, could have expected this level of magic. The Queen of Salix – Despair – had created the army within her enemy. In all of Bastian's long life, he'd never seen anything like it.

"So be it." He straightens. "Come."

"Where are we going?" Nefari asks, defiantly stomping her foot.

Bastian had begun to walk away. He peers over his shoulder. Every set of eyes is on the miniature shadow queen. "To your new home," he says, turning himself to face her once more. "Until you are prepared to fight for your realm, you will live with the centaurs. You will be protected, and in turn, you will train. You will become what this realm will need. You will become the queen your mother couldn't be. And in the end, you will fulfill your Fate."

Rage wrinkles the little girl's nose. He stiffens when the scent of her magic awakens within her.

Wrenchel's words replay in his head. *She will shape the darkness – this Fate-blessed princess of rage and wrath – for she is the crown of endless night and the memory of woeful shadows. Echoes of clinking chain and metal. The sharp sting of leather. The bitter taste of tears will feed despair, but the hopeful shards of a broken kingdom will find the fated queen, and then death will yawn and swallow the realm.*

In this moment, right at this second eight years ago, Nefari Ashcroft was born. And right in this moment, with her magic awakening and the prophecy unfolding . . .

"Happy birthday, Nefari Astra Galazee Ashcroft, Queen of Shadows. Your true fate has begun."

ALSO BY D. FISCHER

| THE CLOVEN PACK SERIES |

| RISE OF THE REALMS SERIES |

| HOWL FOR THE DAMNED |

| HEAVY LIES THE CROWN |

| NIGHT OF TERROR SERIES |

| GRIM FAIRYTALES COLLECTION |

ABOUT THE AUTHOR

Bestselling and award-winning author D. Fischer is a mother of two very busy boys, a wife to a wonderful husband, an owner of two sock-loving german shorthairs, and slave to a rescued cat. Together, they live in Orange City, Iowa.

When D. Fischer isn't chasing after her children, she spends her time typing like a mad woman while consuming vast amounts of caffeine. Known for the darker side of imagination, she enjoys freeing her creativity through worlds that don't exist, no matter how much we wish they did.

Follow D. Fischer on Facebook, Amazon, Bookbub, and Instagram.

DFISCHERAUTHOR.COM